"What would it take to make you cry out, Gem? Have you ever come so hard you forgot everything else?" Damien asked

His bold words jarred her, excited her. They made her realize that, no, Gemma Duncan had never been rocked like a hurricane in her life.

"Don't talk to me like you know me," she said, trying to stay in control of herself. "You don't. Not at all."

"I don't?" He laughed softly. "Certainly I know when a woman wants to be touched. What's your favorite spot, Gem? A long kiss behind the knee? A finger tracing up your spine?" He brushed his mouth over her ear.

Gemma ached, literally hurting because of the burn, the throb inside her. Only pride was keeping her from touching herself.

Because once she stepped over this line with Damien Theroux, there was no going back....

Dear Reader,

What's *your* fantasy?

When Gemma Duncan meets Damien Theroux, this is what he asks her. And—you guessed it—he's more than willing to carry out her most exotic requests. I was lucky to travel the steamy streets of New Orleans in order to flesh out their fantasies: the vivid historical atmosphere, the joie de vivre, the "I'm-willing-to-gain-ten-pounds-for-this-food."

Tough job, but someone has to suffer through it.

The hot-blooded adventures of Damien and Gemma were great fun, and I hope to write many more stories in The Big Easy. I also hope *you* have a good time with this saucy undercover reporter who decides to expose the city's biggest bad boy!

Dare to dream....

Crystal Green

www.crystal-green.com

BORN TO BE BAD

Crystal Green

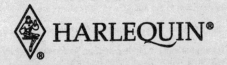

HARLEQUIN®

TORONTO • NEW YORK • LONDON
AMSTERDAM • PARIS • SYDNEY • HAMBURG
STOCKHOLM • ATHENS • TOKYO • MILAN • MADRID
PRAGUE • WARSAW • BUDAPEST • AUCKLAND

To Scott, aka "Duncan":
Thanks for your help with Club Lotus!
Now go out there and conquer the world.

ISBN 0-373-79183-6

BORN TO BE BAD

This edition published by arrangement with Harlequin Books S.A.

www.eHarlequin.com

Printed in U.S.A.

1

IN GEMMA DUNCAN'S FANTASIES, sweat would bead on her skin. It would trickle down her body to dampen the satin sheets while strangers—bad boys who never turned good—trailed their mouths over her belly.

They would dip their tongues into a navel pooled with summer heat, drag their kisses upward, over her writhing torso, her ribs, under the tender swell of her breast, drinking her in. They would never leave their names, but they *would* leave her tapped out physically, filled only with a surging need for more.

Gemma never talked about these fantasies.

But there were safer ones she would share with her new friends over happy-hour cocktails. Fantasies such as winning a Pulitzer at the tender age of twenty-six. Fantasies where she would uncover the nefarious activities of crime lords while crusading as a journalist at the New Orleans *Times-Picayune*. Fantasies where she could bake a perfect soufflé, do a triple axel like Michelle Kwan and come home to a Garden District fantasy mansion full of fantasy puppies saved from the pound with her fantasy fortune.

As far as vivid imaginations went, she was number one. Heck, her fantasies even included knowing how to position a cell phone so that it always received perfect reception.

Needless to say, reality was a little different for Gemma Duncan.

"Jimmy?" she asked for the third time, walking five steps to the left and cocking her head to the right as she exited a French Quarter souvenir store. Taunting her, the phone fuzzed and stuttered in denial.

She'd had her older brother on the line only a second ago. "Jimmy? Can you hear me?"

The shop's zydeco music, with its energetic pulse of percussion and accordion, caused Gemma to plug one ear and wander through the muggy July air toward Dumaine Street. The threat of an afternoon rain braided itself with the smell of battered crawfish and spices from a nearby café.

"Hello?" She clutched her shopping bag, eager to talk to Jimmy and be back on her way to the *Weekly Gossip* offices in the Central Business District. Today she'd been interviewing a psychic who was integral to her latest headline: "Swamp Girl Finds Love with Tarot Reader."

Truly. That was it. This was why Gemma used a pen name—Duncan James—as opposed to her real one.

As she wandered farther down the street, away from the tourists and toward her second destination, a voodoo shop, her older brother's voice squawked in and out of range.

Lunch-hour efficiency, she thought, somewhat proud of her scheduling skills. On Dumaine, she would not only achieve possible reception but also buy gris-gris bag souvenirs for an out-of-town friend. Oh, and then there was the antique shop where she could see if that white-satin-gowned jazz-singer painting was still for sale....

"Jimmy," she said again. "I'm trying to... Aw, forget it. If you can hear me, I'm running errands anyway, so I bought that grotesque shellacked baby gator head for your wife. I'll send it priority mail tomorrow, okay? By the way, tell her happy birthday, you sicko. If *I* had a husband with a yen for weird gag gifts like you, there'd be some damage. And I say that with all the love in my heart. Talk to you later."

In one last, hopeful attempt to achieve reception, Gemma paced near a courtyard. It had a wrought-iron gate, and banana-tree leaves that leaned over the brick wall like a bored woman passing time while watching the street's infrequent traffic. Beyond the barriers, a man's raised voice competed with Jimmy's tinny bark.

"Gemma, I heard that. When you finally get it into your thick head that you've moved to the wrong city, and listen to your family and move back here—"

Oops. Not...understanding...a...word...you...say...."

She snapped shut her cell phone, tucked it into the purse she'd slung crosswise over her chest and rested her spine against the courtyard bricks. She wiped at the heat steaming the straight tendrils of her upswept hair into curlicues while the man's disembodied voice continued to bluster behind the wall. A fountain tinkled in the background.

Water. The splashes reminded her of Orange County,

California, where the dog days of summer were tempered by beach winds and afternoons by the swimming pool.

But that's not where she belonged. She'd visited New Orleans and had never left, especially after the *Weekly Gossip* job had come along. The tabloid had sounded good because she'd been desperate for income and experience.

Besides, the "Big Easy" had always sounded adventurous, a bit scary. Naughty.

The last place anyone who knew "nice" Gemma Duncan would've expected her to end up.

Over the courtyard wall, another male voice had joined the first one. Gemma idly closed her eyes, listening, lulled by the southern afternoon sounds.

"You're playing with some fire, here, Mr. Lamont. I'll leave now, before our meeting humiliates you further."

Gemma's eyes eased open, lured by the second man's voice. His tone had the rough undertow of a bayou night, where unknown dangers were hidden by darkness, the buzz of crickets, the lap of black water against crumbling docks.

A warm ache shocked her lower belly, then pulsed lower, urging her to press her thighs together. Man, if a mere voice could get her going, she really needed a date. Maybe it was time to start meeting more people and doing less work.

People such as...

She strained to hear him again, that echo of her fantasies—shadow-edged and wild, with just a hint of foreign danger.

Right, she thought. Only in my craziest dreams.

Most disappointingly, the first man was talking again, his N'awlins accent charged with anger. "You rigged that roulette wheel and bled me last night. Did you invite me to that gaming room with ruination in mind, Theroux?"

Theroux? She knew that name.

An intimidating pause spoke volumes, and she could imagine the accuser, Lamont, backing up a few steps.

"Anything else?" Theroux asked. "After all, you invited me to meet with you alone, and I expected to deal in some true business with a man of your stature. But your threats don't interest me, Lamont. Neither does your desperation."

"I resigned from the company three months ago, so you can't hold anything against me now." Lamont's voice shook a little. "I've become a better man."

"After you've tasted what your employees had to endure? I think so."

"What are you, Theroux? Some self-appointed avenger? Yes? I lost a lot of money in your joint. I could—"

"But you won't. You'll keep your voice down and go back to your home unruffled. Understand?"

Had Theroux stolen from this Lamont? And what was all this talk about employees and revenge?

Heart fluttering during the ensuing hesitation, Gemma shrank away from the gate, sheltering herself behind the brick wall. Maybe she should leave, but her inner journalist wouldn't allow it. Sometimes the best stories were the ones you stumbled over.

Damien Theroux was gossip gold, a city legend. A fixture in the good-old-boy network.

Just by picturing what kind of man went with that kind of voice, she grew a little feverish.

Was he suave? Graying at the temples? As bearish as Tony Soprano?

While she considered it, Theroux's victim, Lamont, was no doubt taking a moment to gather himself. He finally responded with more respect. "All I want is my money back, Mr. Theroux. I've worked hard for it."

"Not as hard as I did. And, rest assured, the proceeds will go to a proper place."

"Please!" Lamont's voice cracked. "I'll have to sell my home, you realize."

More silence cut through the humidity, and Gemma held her breath. The brick wall scratched against her cheek as she slipped down an inch, knee joints turning to liquid.

This was ridiculous, hiding like a child. Eavesdropping. But she couldn't leave. *Wouldn't* leave.

Heavy footsteps neared the gate. With a guilty start, Gemma opened her eyes, then darted behind a long, exhausted bronze Buick parked streetside. She held her crinkling plastic souvenir bag against her thigh, hoping it wouldn't make another sound.

She'd hit rock bottom, spying like this.

As the iron gate moaned open, Lamont's tortured voice echoed the rusty hinges. "You're not getting away with this. You are not all-powerful, Damien Theroux!"

Damien Theroux. Confirmation that this was the shady man she'd read about in the newspapers.

She could hear Theroux's steps come to a halt.

"I wish I had the power of gods," he said. "Then I'd fleece you in the afterlife, too, when we're both in hell."

Oh, what a quote *that*'d make. Gemma only wished she had her tiny recorder on.

From the sound of it, Lamont was getting braver, closer, as if he was at the gate, too. "Wouldn't the public love to know about these *other* dealings? Your weaknesses? I think a few of your competitors read the papers, if you catch my meaning."

Theroux merely laughed—but not because he was entertained, obviously. Or maybe he was.

By now, Gemma's head was swimming. This could lead to a real story. Maybe an exposé of one of New Orleans's most intriguing characters?

Her ticket to respect.

If she could just find out exactly what these "other" dealings were.

After the seemingly endless lack of response, Theroux spoke. "I think you're too smart to talk about my business, Mr. Lamont, if you catch *my* meaning."

That must have done the trick for Lamont because Theroux continued swinging open the gate. He shut it with finality and walked away.

Oh, thank God, thank God, thank God he hadn't seen her crouched by the Buick.

As she waited a beat, a car drove by. Nonchalantly, Gemma flashed a smile at the miffed driver while he watched her hiding.

When he'd passed, she paused another moment, peeking around the car, watching an overweight, bald man—Lamont—as he trudged back toward his foliage-obscured brick home. Moments later, he slammed his door.

Quivering with the buzz of career success, Gemma peeked around the other side of the Buick, focusing on a tall, broad-shouldered, wiry figure as he moved down the street with the walk of a predator—slightly hunched, wary.

He had black shoulder-length hair that echoed the lazy wisps of a fine cigar's smoke. Hair that reminded her of a hallway in the dead of night when you have to drag a hand along the walls to find your way. A hallway where something might be waiting for you to pass, to feel the smile on its face when you discover it's there.

Was she going to pursue this? Damien Theroux wasn't a woman who lived in the sticks, professing to be a swamp thing in love with a psychic. He wasn't anyone else she usually wrote about, either—not the reincarnated Elvises or the women who claimed to be the next Marie Laveau.

Damien Theroux was her chance to make it big, to be taken seriously by everyone who'd expected more out of her than tabloid reporting. Even herself.

Hell, *yeah,* she was going to do this.

Gemma slyly removed herself from behind the Buick, trailing Theroux's panther stride, his black designer suit, the brightness of her future.

He rounded onto Royal Street, and she took care to act like a tourist, gawking at brightly hued buildings with their jolly paint-flaked shutters, the lacy iron fences, stray drops from this morning's rain shower dripping on her head from galleries and balconies.

As Theroux moved onto St. Philip, the streets grew more deserted. Gemma wondered if she should stay on the beaten paths, if she'd entered an area that concierges warned their hotel guests to stay away from.

A hungover man without shoes told her in passing that he'd fallen asleep in front of a bar and someone had stolen his wallet and boots, and she just about turned right back around to safer territory.

"Brave Reporter Breaks Open the Truth About Notorious Criminal!" screamed the headlines of her mind.

She kept going.

Finally, Theroux disappeared into a crumbling, two-story wooden dwelling that squatted on a corner. The word *Cuffs* was painted in green over the awning-shrouded door.

Cuffs, huh? Gemma grinned, liking the place already. Her California-suburb family and friends would be shocked, but she was curious.

Not that she'd ever admit that out loud.

As she ventured closer, she wondered if this was Theroux's place. Everyone knew the man owned aboveboard businesses such as restaurants, bars and souvenir shops. Ironically, he was said to own the exact store where she'd purchased the gator head today.

But she was more interested in *other* establishments—especially the ones Lamont had mentioned.

Gemma took a big breath, fortifying herself. She could barely even walk straight with all the adrenaline attacking her system.

When she finally made it inside, she didn't have long to absorb the murky atmosphere—the T-shirted, buzzcutted, beefy men clutching the handles of mugs and watching a TV game show at the four-sided bar. The smell of booze and perspiration mixed by the slow blades of a ceiling fan. The clank of balls rolling over a pool table in the far corner.

Instead, a pair of strong arms engulfed her with the quickness of a flashing bite. One hand sprawled over her belly, pressing her back into a hard, lean body covered in linen. The other gripped her chin, turning her face toward her captor while he guided her into a deserted corner.

Theroux.

Only now, this close, could she see the feral glow of his pale blue eyes set against skin the color of a tobacco leaf.

Gemma tried to bite into his hand, but he loosened his hold while refusing to let go. Mouth quirked, his smile was mean, his gaze was narrowed.

"It's not nice to follow people, *chérie*."

Fear choked her throat, and she was painfully aware that her only weapon was a dime-store gator head wrapped in a plastic bag. Her heart jackhammered in her chest. He could feel her crazy pulse, couldn't he?

This wasn't a fantasy anymore.

Something shifted in his eyes, the shards of a broken kaleidoscope changing form. He released her, except for the fingers that kept a hold of her skirt waistband.

God, she couldn't breathe. She couldn't run, either.

Yet, inexplicably, she took a step toward him.

His heavy eyebrows shot up. His half smile returned.

Her instinctive response had caught her unaware, also. But Gemma gathered all her courage and shed her old skin—the girl next door who'd made the honor roll and the dean's list throughout school. The editor of every academic newspaper she'd worked on. Her family's great hope.

She shot a cheeky glance at his hand. His fingers had gone from grasping her waistband to settling on her hip, his thumb looped inside the skirt's rim.

Now that she could breathe again, she detected his scent—cool, mysterious, brandied.

"Do you mind?" she asked, directing her glance from his encroaching hand to his face.

"I mind being tailed, yeah," he said. "Is there something you want? My day's been full of demands, anyway."

Didn't she know it. "Your hand's still on me."

"So it is."

His smile widened, but it wasn't playful. No, this was what sin looked like when it was amused.

Gemma's blood rushed downward, making her stir uncomfortably. Making the inside of her thighs slick with the excitement of the chase. Making her swell and throb.

Dammit, she needed this story, and the enigmatic Damien Theroux was right here, ready for the unmasking.

She wasn't going to lose this chance.

Instead, she stilled the trembling in her lower stomach, hoping it wouldn't travel to her limbs.

It did.

But her voice was strong, even as she played dumb. "You own this place?"

He merely stared at her.

"I take that as a yes."

"Take it any way you want it."

Her appreciation for the art of a good double entendre tickled her nerves. Luckily, she found her steel again.

"I was wondering…" *what you'd feel like inside me* "…if there were any openings. You know, for a waitress."

Genius, she thought. Working for him would be a good way to gather some sly information about these "other" dealings Lamont had hinted at.

But Theroux just continued staring.

"No?" she asked.

His thumb unhooked from her waistband, coasting lower, brushing over the center of her belly. Gemma jerked and grabbed his wrist as a bolt of desire shot through her. With emphatic meaning, she pushed his hand away.

"We're not hiring," he said. "For waitresses."

Gemma gulped, dreading her next question.

HAVING GROWN UP IN A DOWN-at-the-heels section of the Faubourg Marigny, Damien had been raised to watch his own back. That's why, halfway through his trip from Lamont's, he'd been aware of someone following him. Usually, he kept much better track of his surroundings, but today he'd been distracted by Lamont's threats to go to the media with what he knew. None of Damien's marks had ever been that stupid.

Would Lamont actually chance it?

Damien highly doubted so, because the price was too high. Still, he didn't like being targeted. Trailed. You always felt it in your spine—the watching. The way a potential threat sought out your vulnerable spots.

And blondes like this woman standing in front of him were one of his biggest weaknesses.

Now, as she glanced up at him with those baby-doll-blue eyes, Damien knew better than to let down his guard for the second time that day.

She had Barbie packaging, but the innocence of her heart-shaped face was thrown out of whack by a surprisingly square jaw. Delicate, to be sure, but still strong.

"So," she said, cool as a mint sprig in an iced cocktail, "what kind of work *is* available here?"

He ran a gaze over her body, starting from the flats of her sensible shoes upward—the long, tanned legs, the career-girl khaki skirt that covered slim hips and a trim waist, the humidity-soaked blue top that clung to a pair of small, rounded breasts. As his attention lingered there, her nipples hardened, pebbling the material in two strategic locations.

Deliberately, he returned his focus to her face. Her cheeks were flushed, probably because she was insulted. Either that or... Could she be turned on by his interest?

Did this girl play dirty? And had her game started when she'd followed him here?

Lust speared through Damien, a raging grumble reaching from gut to cock. He could play dirty, too. In fact, that's the only way he wanted it. Dirty, and easy to dust off.

"What kind of work do you do?" he asked.

"Waitressing."

"And?"

She pursed those lips. Blow-job lips, as he'd grown up calling them. "I'm not sure I understand, Mr....?"

"I'm asking about your experience, Ms....?" He mocked her by grinning.

Refusing to back down, she laughed. "Call me Gem. Gem...James."

She rested a hand on her hip, and Damien ached, remembering how his palm had molded those curves.

"I waitressed at an Italian restaurant in high school. In college, I worked at the same trendy bar for four years. I've also done time at a few chain restaurants recently. So what do you say? Are you hiring?"

"No."

She glanced at the floor, but not before Damien saw a flash of disappointment. When she looked back up, she was giving him the puppy-dog treatment.

"I swear, I'm a great server."

Was she now?

He must've been wearing the happiest grin he could manage, because she perked up. "I really need a job. I moved out here a few months ago, and I haven't gotten on my feet yet. I'll work my ass off for this place."

"That'd be a shame, because even though I've only seen the front of you, I expect the back to be just as divine."

She gasped slightly, and her eyelashes lowered over an appraising gaze, not because he'd offended her, Damien guessed, but because he'd broken her code. Unlocked her.

Again, he wondered if she'd come into Cuffs for more than a waitressing job.

It wouldn't be the first time a woman had wandered into one of his establishments seeking to test the rumors about Damien Theroux. There were females who liked the taste of bad boys, and he was only too happy to oblige when the need suited him.

Truth to tell, he thought, moving forward, looming over her, it suited him now.

Eyes a hazy blue, her soft lips parted, forcing him to stifle a pleased groan at the thought of how they'd feel on his penis. Without thinking, he slipped his hand into her waistband again, knuckles skimming against her hip bone. He pulled her closer, his cock hardening.

For a second, neither of them moved. But within the blink of an eye, she recovered, cleared her throat, backed away. He kept a hold of her silk tank top, not wanting to let go. The material slithered out of her skirt.

Damn, how he wanted to help her out of the rest of those clothes.

As he rubbed the sinuous material between his thumb and forefinger, she ignored the gesture, acting as if it wasn't happening. Her aloofness got him worked up because he couldn't get a bead on this woman.

Outside, rain started to patter on the roof.

"Why would you want to work at Cuffs, anyway?" he asked in a low voice, as if they were in a bedroom, three inches away from a mattress. "Why don't you go to Hooters? Crescent City Brewhouse? Somewhere 'trendier'?"

To her credit, she didn't back down. "I like the name. Cuffs. What exactly does it mean?"

Should he tell her it was an homage to the retired cops and blue-collar fellows who liked to hang out here?

"Use your imagination," he said instead.

"Well, you're not one for hiding behind social niceties, are you?"

"Never." Not since his dad had gotten worked over. Not since Martin Theroux had died from the shame brought on by the ruins of his life. Not since his son had decided that being bad was the only way to live good.

"You're not the type of guy who'd take pity on a woman in need and hire her out of the kindness of your heart?"

"Not as a waitress."

"Then what…? Oh."

There it went. The lightbulb. That's right, Damien thought. Think the worst.

New Orleans cathouses were notorious, especially with men who dealt in Damien's area. He didn't know if Gem realized he ran a private gaming room in addition to his legitimate businesses, but going along with her assumption that he engaged in illicit dealings didn't bother him in the least.

Prostitution and drugs were part of the scene. They drew in customers, served as perks. Gaming downstairs, sex upstairs. That's how it worked.

Except for Damien. He was in it for the "marks"—victims—and the fleecing. Not that anyone needed to know why he kept his gaming clean of hookers and dope.

The more horrible his reputation, the easier it would be for him to survive.

"I'm not…" Gem gestured with her hands, waving them somewhere around her chest. "You know…"

"That sort of girl?"

She didn't say anything.

Their gazes caught, and something unspoken passed from her to him. His blood jolted in his veins, warming, boiling.

What the hell was she about?

"Damien!"

He let go of Gem's shirt, knowing that voice. "Roxy."

A buxom redhead with streaks of gray framing her elfin features sauntered over to the dark corner, a jaded gleam in her eyes. "Who's this here?"

"Ms. James was just leaving."

"I'm needing help, you fool." Roxy grabbed Gem's hand, tugging the young woman toward her. "I heard the two of you. She asks for a job, and you putter around the subject. Look at her, would you. She's what our customers like—pretty and young. I tell you, Damien Theroux, no more interviews for you. Stick to the upstairs work."

"Yes, ma'am." He gave her a lazy salute. Only two people in the world could ever talk to him like this— Roxy and his *maman*, bless her soul. Everyone else could go to the devil.

With a long-suffering sigh, Roxy took Gem's hand and placed it between both of hers. "You need a job, baby, here it is. I'm shorthanded since Eva quit days ago, and Damien could care less. I hope you can look past him and be my savior?"

Gem's smile almost lit the room. Damien sucked in a breath, then moved away, creating distance.

"Thank you, thank you, thank you!" Gem hugged the older woman, then clapped her hands once. "When do I start?"

"How 'bout now? Our busy time is some hours away, and I'll want you up and running. We'll consider this a test run tonight. How does that sound?"

"Great. *I'll* be great. But may I make one quick phone call first?"

"Please." Roxy snapped an impertinent glance to Damien, then shook her moneymaker in the direction of the bar. Gem herself gave him her own saucy look and made her way toward the entrance.

Damien watched her go, noting that her ass definitely was divine, just as he'd predicted. Firm and full in all the right places.

Before he did something ill-advised, he headed out of the bar and toward the stairs leading to his office. So Roxy had taken his departed *maman*'s place once again. Nice for her. Now Damien had a screwable waitress who could provide a few nights of distraction.

And he certainly needed it.

As Damien settled down to his desk to shuffle through his accounts, he lost himself in his work, happy to see what a profit he was making.

Happy to find his next victim so he could bleed the worst men dry.

2

WHEN GEMMA GOT BACK TO the *Weekly Gossip* that afternoon, she was pumped up, and it wasn't just because she wanted to pitch the story of the decade to her editor.

Damien Theroux had done something to her. Flipped a switch, pushed a button…something to turn on the inner furnace.

Even now, as she sat in front of her editor's desk, she couldn't shake the feeling of Theroux's thumb while it slid along her stomach, the drag of her silk top whispering out of her skirt as he tugged it toward him.

But this wasn't the time for daydreaming, or for ducking into a restroom stall to press her fingers between her thighs to assuage the throb of excitement.

This was the time to finally rock and roll.

"So I trained for a couple of hours at Cuffs," she said, relating the afternoon's events to Nancy Mendoza, editor in chief, "and I'm in like Flynn with the head waitress, Roxy. The job is comparable to riding a bike. All those pizzas and beers I served in the past amount to a perfect cover."

"Gemma…"

"I'm going back tonight, and that's when I'll really

put the pedal to the metal. See, I want to find out about these 'other' dealings Lamont mentioned. We all know about the Damien Theroux in the papers, but what drives this man? How did he get into a life of gambling, drugs and prostitution? And if I could talk to people who know him and work for him, or sneak upstairs to chat with a couple of his girls—"

"Gemma!"

She stopped, mouth open to deliver another round of plans. From the corner of her eye, she could see through the office's window. The other tabloid reporters punched away at their keyboards or stared at their computer screens.

She wouldn't be one of their kind for much longer. No how, no way.

Nancy braced her hands against her desk, probably gearing up to break Gemma's spirit. Again. It happened with every idea that didn't exactly "fit" into the *Weekly Gossip*'s pages.

Holding up a hand, Gemma interrupted. "I know what you're going to say. 'Go back to your human-interest stories, Gemma.'"

"You're good at them. Very good."

"Is that why they're referred to as 'freaks and geeks' pieces?" Gemma sighed. "Where's the dignity for the subjects? And for me?"

Nancy's brown eyes went soft with understanding. Every once in a while, when the editor tippled a drink or two at Friday happy hour, she'd lose her armor and tell Gemma that she'd never expected to work on a tabloid publication, either.

Funny. How many people actually did end up with the life they'd pictured while doodling on their Pee-Chee folders during high school algebra?

"Leave Damien Theroux for *60 Minutes* or the newspapers," Nancy said. Her brown hair was in a tight bun, and she was wearing her typical uniform of a crisp button-down and gray skirt. Her efficient manner had won her the nickname The General. "Theroux is beyond our scope."

"An exposé on Theroux would take this publication places we've never been." Gemma couldn't help arguing. This story had reached epic proportions in her mind. "Imagine. We're a national publication. If we could reveal even half of this city's corruption to Molly Supermarket Mom of the Heartland, that would be the first step. The story would be picked up by more prestigious mainstream publications because, of course, it'll be so well researched by me. A drop of water won't even be able to slip through my reporting, the corroboration and evidence will be so tight. Heck, maybe we'll even be getting calls from Bill O'Reilly or Diane Sawyer to consult on their shows...."

The four-star General hadn't stopped her, and that was encouraging. Gemma allowed the dreams to dangle between the two of them for a moment as the editor covered her mouth with an ink-stained hand. The woman tapped a finger, deliberating.

Time for the coup de grâce. "Damien Theroux is Pulitzer material."

Nancy uncovered her mouth to reveal a reluctant smile, miraculously devoid of black smudges. But the positive sign disappeared quickly.

"This isn't our typical headline."

"Dream big, Mendoza!"

The editor held up a finger. "If he sued for libel, he'd decimate us. Or maybe he'd do worse, based on his reputation. Rumor has it that he's got ties to the mob."

"I'm not afraid. And you're not talking like a journalist."

Pow. Gemma could see the damage in Nancy's gaze. Any self-respecting reporter put the truth above all else.

Gemma continued. "Even if I've only worked with you a couple of months, I know we're both more than the *Weekly Gossip* allows us to be, Nancy. This is our big shot, and you can depend on me to get it right."

"You're not brassy enough for this."

Gemma gulped, hearing the judgment of her first real editor on the day she'd gotten fired. *You've got no guts, Duncan.*

With more humility, she said, "You should've seen me this afternoon. You would've been proud. I gave Theroux as good as I got from him."

"Oh, Gemma." Nancy leaned over her desk, more a budding friend than an editor. "Right now, I just want to tell you to go back home and forget about this. We're talking about the underworld, here. It's not the Lalaurie haunted house or a story about UFOs. This is real."

Gemma pounded on the arms of her chair. "So is my need to investigate this man."

She pressed her lips together, regretting the outburst.

Yes, she was desperate. Among other things, she hated the way her family defined her career. Years ago, when she'd been an eager cub reporter at the *Orange*

County Register, they'd bragged about her in Christmas newsletters. Now, they told their friends that she was "in between jobs." And that was true enough, because she didn't intend to write below her ability forever.

"Hey." Nancy reached out, laid a hand on Gemma's. "You all right?"

Actually, no. She hadn't been since she'd gotten canned at the *Register.* What a blow—being scooped on a pivotal story about a sleazy politician because she'd been too mousy to pursue every angle.

"I'm fine," Gemma said, forcing a grin, "if you give me a chance with this. I won't let you down."

Nancy sat back and expelled a huge breath. Behind her on the white wall, *Weekly Gossip* covers screamed headlines: "Miracle Baby Saves Whale!" and "Wronged Wife Takes Gory Revenge on Hubby!"

Tilting her head to an almost beggarly angle, Gemma burned with hope. *Please say yes.*

The editor crossed her arms over her chest. "I'll give you two weeks to turn up something solid and marketable on Theroux. Something explosive we don't already know about him. And if it looks good…"

Gemma's pulse started racing.

"Plus," Nancy added, "you keep your day job here, writing about your 'freaks and geeks.'"

At this point, Gemma would've agreed to do a naked Irish jig on a float during Mardi Gras. "Will do!"

When she stood, latent doubt twisted through her conscience. She was about to go undercover to dig up some dirt on an unsuspecting man. A man who'd touched her with arrogant heat, and burned her body from the inside out this afternoon. There would be no straightforward questions, no honesty with him.

Once again, his hungry gaze consumed her, making her blood sing.

Did she really have the guts to layer lie upon lie to him? To disrupt a man's life by offering it bare for the world to see? Was she really that ruthless?

Sure. If rumor was correct, this bad boy deserved his comeuppance. Reporters lived to see justice dealt to men like him. Right?

Right.

Gemma opened Nancy's door, newly invigorated. "Needless to say, I'm working nights now. I can't come over for a movie and daiquiris tomorrow."

"I guess I'll have to keep Russell Crowe all to myself, then." Nancy waved Gemma out. "Go. You've got a story due. And, Gemma? As your friend, I'm telling you to be careful."

"I've got it under control, *chica*. Chill."

Then, with a tiny wave, she left, heading straight for her desk.

She'd actually gotten the green light for this story! Sort of. More like a yellow light, but she was still ready to go.

Even if she ended up ruining Theroux's life.

Somewhat torn, she arrived at her workstation to find it cluttered with more than notes for her most recent project.

Every office has a pain in the ass, and Waller Smith was the designated hemorrhoid for the *Weekly Gossip*. A snore ripped out of him while he slumped in Gemma's padded chair, his ash-blond hair ruffled and in sore need of a cut, his scuffed Bruno Magli knockoffs propped near her keyboard, his gumbo-stained button-down and crumpled tie as washed out as the green of his bloodshot eyes—when they were open. When she'd first met him, her first impression had been of a sun-cooked Robert Redford. But Gemma now knew better.

She managed to ignore him while simultaneously guiding his feet off her desk.

The shift of position awakened him. He blinked at her, focusing. "Duncan." Then he stretched, a canary-eating grin on his face. "Kissing up to our chief again?"

"Anything to get your panties in a wad, Smith. I believe you're in my chair?"

Waller acted surprised to be sitting there. "Well, pardon my butt."

Yawning to a stand, he offered her the seat with a grand gesture. Then, with deadline purpose, she pretended to get to work, but Waller wasn't leaving.

"What can I do for you?" she finally asked, giving him a smile that one usually reserves for a salesman who rings the doorbell during dinner.

"Reaching a little high for your talents, aren't you?"

The comment felt like a sucker punch. "Aren't you the last person to be judging talent? Since you don't have any yourself, I mean?"

An indefinable emotion passed over Smith's face, and Gemma wanted to take her smart-ass comment back. Actually, that really wasn't true. He was exasperating, and deserved a return helping of everything he dished out.

Not that Smith probably cared about what she'd said

to him. He had a way of not giving a tinker's damn about anything.

"Duncan, congratulations. You're growing a spine. Now all you need to be a decent reporter is the ability to read lips, which I was doing a few minutes ago. Ah, the miracle of office windows."

"You...?" Gemma stopped herself, remembering some sort of happy-hour rumor about Smith having a deaf sister.

With the smug laziness of a sunning gator, he leaned against another reporter's empty desk. "It's easy to distinguish the name 'Theroux' on a woman's lips. So you overheard him and a crony arguing today?"

"You tell me."

"Yes, you did. And you think, sweet little thing, that you'll be the one pen-slinging warrior who'll hit his heel and bring him down." He shook his shaggy head. "Another well-meaning crusader bites the dust."

"Don't you have work to do?"

"Sure, but there's always enough time to write about sleaze and sex at my desk. I'm more interested in how you're going to survive."

Gemma accessed her waiting story in the computer. "How adorable. You're fixated on my safety."

"I said I'm *interested*."

His meaning dug into her skin. She whipped around in her chair to face him. "You've got your own assignments, so don't even think about mine. Concentrate on those cheating wives and crimes of passion. I'm busy."

For a second, it seemed like Smith himself wanted to be writing about more than tabloid fodder, too. But this was Waller Smith, the guy who wandered in an hour late every day, then alternated power naps with every other sentence he punched into his computer. This was a "reporter" who mindlessly reached his word count, collected his check and called it a day.

He proved Gemma right by shrugging and ambling away, but not before he said, "Watch your back, Duncan. In every direction."

Was that a warning about Theroux or Smith?

Feeling surrounded, Gemma cleared her mind and attacked her story.

She'd get her man. No matter what her co-worker—or her conscience—said, Damien Theroux was all hers.

As the sun chased the rain from the sky, then disappeared beyond the horizon itself, customers walked into a swanky, jazz-soaked restaurant two blocks off the well-worn paths of the French Quarter.

Some came to Club Lotus to eat the contemporary Creole food—the almond-crusted soft-shell crab, the turtle soup, the shrimp remoulade. Some came to listen to a saxophone mixing with a moody bass guitar.

But the ones who'd received crystal markers etched with a panther from the bartenders who worked in Damien Theroux's other establishments had come to gamble.

The process was easy, just like the city itself. If you had a lot of money—or if you didn't mind losing what you had of it—you would be invited to the hidden game room. On designated nights, you would dress in elegant clothing, stroll through Club Lotus and its tables of curious diners, go straight back to the waiting elevator. There, you would drop your crystal marker down the chute and wait for an employee to send up the car.

After taking the elevator down, feeling your pockets weighted with money you hoped to double, you would emerge into another world—one that not every person was fortunate enough to frequent.

In Theroux's gaming establishment, you would find burgundy walls lined by mahogany wood, a fortified room with a small window where you would exchange your money for chips and ceiling fans that cut into the smoke from gratis Cuban cigars, the Cristal and brandy fumes. You would scent the sweat from gamblers who weren't having much luck.

You would search among the one-armed bandits for the tables—blackjack, poker, roulette and craps— picking your game for the night. As the music of clanking chips and slot songs urged you on, you would settle at that poker table, knowing you were bound to win.

A hostess might ask if you needed anything, but she wouldn't be talking about women or nose candy. Not at Theroux's place. You were here to win money, to take advantage of the high-dollar markers that legal casinos didn't offer.

No limits.

Tonight would be your night.

An hour into your game, as your pile of chips grew into several columns, you would see the man himself walking the exposed upper floor, trailing his hand along the railing, dressed in a tailored suit as black as his reputation. When he nodded, you would return the gesture.

After all, you would be taking Damien Theroux's money home, and he deserved your appreciation.

DAMIEN TORE HIS GAZE FROM the nodding man at the poker table and strolled to a corner of the upper floor, where Jean Dulac, a childhood friend who wore a ready smile and Armani threads, awaited him. Jean's dark brown hair was spiky, a bit wild, but the man's pedigree was much slicker. He was the son of the local mob boss.

"I see that tonight's bird knows you're here," Jean said.

Damien didn't need to look at the poker tables again, but Jean did, locking on to the latest retired CEO to grace the room. Gerald O'Shea, former chief executive officer of Havishau Corporations, had gotten rich off the sweat of his employees by helping himself to a few generous bonuses while bankrupting the company. Consequently, the peons who'd worked for him were suddenly left without jobs or retirement accounts.

Men like O'Shea were the reason this gaming establishment existed. Damien took their crimes personally.

"I kind of like this moment. The calm before the storm that sweeps the bird into its own trap." He extracted two cards from the lining of his Versace jacket. "See. Twenty-one, Jean. I hit the big hand this morning."

His friend ignored Damien's reference to a ritual— superstitiously drawing cards at the crack of dawn to predict if the day would be a winner...or a loser.

"Don't underestimate your feelings. I'd say you relish this, Damien." Jean shook his head. "Too much, if you ask me."

"Who did ask?"

"Sorry for having a history with you. I thought maybe I was allowed to give a damn, considering we used to raise some hell together."

"You're worried?"

"Concerned."

"I've got Roxy for that." Damien shot a sidelong look down at Jean. "As long as you and your papa get a cut from tonight's take, there shouldn't be a problem. Life remains good."

As Damien focused on O'Shea again, he could feel the burden of his friend's gaze on him. Jean had helped him through *Papa*'s mortification, his suicide, the years of poverty when he and his mother had eaten ketchup mixed with water—*soup*, she'd called it—and beyond.

In fact, Jean was one big reason Damien was able to run the gaming room during this, its first year, with minimal suffering. Armand Dulac, Jean's father—and a few key local law-enforcement officials, among others—took a percentage of Damien's profit and made sure he was left alone to do business. Since Armand had mentored Damien from poverty to success, the good-old-boy network took care of Theroux, spreading the word that he wasn't to be touched.

Jean leaned on the railing. "I wish you would get out of this pattern, Damien. Me? I have no choice. I'm to take over for the old man one day. But you don't need the money from gaming. Not with your other holdings."

"You know my other businesses don't take care of O'Shea's or Lamont's ilk. Here, they get what they deserve."

Here, Damien took the money the CEOs had stolen from their companies. Here, he made certain the screwed employees got *their* cut.

Jean's pause was ripping at Damien. His judgment hurt.

"All of this won't bring your father back," Jean said.

"Nothing will." Damien stuffed his twenty-one— ace of spades and queen of hearts—back into his jacket. "But watching O'Shea take a fall right now makes me feel a lot better."

As Jean sighed and said his good-nights, Damien dismissed his faint sense of guilt and felt the first stirrings of comfort. He'd set up O'Shea, to be sure, researching him, making certain one of his bartenders would present the man with a crystal invitation, then hoping he would be tempted to increase his ill-gotten savings by showing up tonight.

At the moment, a few of Damien's employees were loitering behind O'Shea at the poker table, signaling the dealer as to what cards he held. The other table players also worked for Damien, and a hostess was keeping him up-to-date on O'Shea's incredible run of good luck.

Incredible. Not really. Damien just wanted him to get cocky before the big fall.

Before he gave the signal to start bleeding the ex-CEO, he took a minute to remember his *papa*.

Damien's boyhood hero lived on the back of his eyelids. At night, he'd only have to attempt sleep to see him again. Now, he pictured *Papa*—a kindly, sideburn-wearing man who'd taught him how to fish and play Hearts—standing on the opposite side of the table from O'Shea, dealing the cards that would ruin him.

With the slight lift of Damien's index finger, an employee caught the signal. O'Shea's luck was about to change.

Settling against the railing to watch, Damien's jaw tightened, his hands fisted.

Someone came to stand next to him, waiting patiently to be noticed.

Damn it all. "Yes?"

When Damien looked over, he saw it was Kumbar, his stocky, dusky-skinned security pro. Next to him stood another security expert—a new guy who looked quite nervous to be in the presence of the big boss. As usual, Kumbar allowed someone else to do all the talking.

"Mr. Rollins is back," the other man said. "Blackjack. He's losing pretty big."

Rollins. A neighborhood antique-store owner who'd been having financial problems lately. An honest man.

"How'd he get a marker?" Damien asked.

"I'll check it out, sir."

In order to emphasize his underling's promise, Kumbar allowed himself the expansive luxury of a lethargic nod.

Damien shook his head. "People like Rollins aren't supposed to be in here."

But they always found their way somehow.

Thudding a fist against the railing while glaring at

O'Shea's table, Damien saw tonight's victim frown as he surrendered his first pile of chips.

With a spark of satisfaction, Damien dismissed the security worker to check on Rollins. That left Kumbar.

"It's things like this that bring a business down," Damien said.

Kumbar gave a firm nod.

"Last night's mark—you recall Lamont?—threatened to go to the press."

Kumbar jerked a thumb toward Jean, who was saying his farewells to an attractive cocktail server on the floor. Damien knew what his right-hand man was asking: had he told his best friend—the mob boss's son—about Lamont's threat?

"The last thing I want to do is get a bird killed, Kumbar. I hesitate to even tell you. I'm certain Lamont won't say a word. When I left him, he looked scared as a rabbit. No, I think more about what could happen if someone braver did tell the media about how this place really works. Where the money goes."

Another Kumbar nod.

Damien didn't want to say it out loud. He cherished his dark reputation; it kept him from being touched, destroyed by the competition. It was the more critical dealings Lamont had referred to that would get Damien into trouble.

It was what he did with most of the profits after the cash was shuttled out of the casino, taken to a counting house, then laundered through one of his souvenir shops.

"My image is what protects me," Damien said instead. "I'd like it to stay as poisonous as possible."

Kumbar glanced at the blackjack tables, and Damien's gaze followed. There sat Mike Rollins, sweating, arms protecting a few scattered chips.

He shouldn't go soft on him. That wasn't how to run a gaming operation. Still, the way the older man slumped in his seat....

His father used to wear the same expression after he'd lost all his money, too.

"Go to him," Damien said. "Get him out of here and find a way to give him back what he lost. Quietly, without him suspecting. Maybe someone shows up in his store tomorrow and buys that expensive white elephant he can't sell. Make sure he knows he's not welcome back."

Kumbar took off to do his duty.

God, Damien thought, I'm an easy sell.

He couldn't revive the interest in watching O'Shea get fleeced. Not now. But there'd be other crooked men, so the lack of entertainment didn't bother Damien so much.

Instead, he decided to go back to Cuffs, because now that he thought about it, there was a certain new waitress there who might be able to take his mind off his troubles.

His body steamed up just picturing Gem James, with her pinned-up Brigitte Bardot hair, her wide blue eyes.

If he couldn't watch O'Shea fall on his back tonight, he'd settle for a woman instead.

3

GEMMA HADN'T FORGOTTEN how exhausting being a waitress was.

Roxy had told her that the help wore high, strappy black pumps, short black skirts and the tightest tank tops in creation. No stranger to a nightlife wardrobe, Gemma had pieced together a decent serving ensemble, complete with a small apron and a black top decorated with silver studs and a skull and crossbones.

So, she had a thing for pirates.

Now, as Aerosmith played on a corner jukebox, she served drinks to a mellow crowd of cops, local blue-collar men and a contingent of hip, artsy types who sat in the corner booths. She was counting the minutes until her first break. Then she could rest her aching tootsies as well as her tray arm.

Past midnight, Roxy finally caught Gemma after she'd delivered a round of Hurricanes to a table of slumming lawyers.

"Those fellows aren't our usual crowd," Roxy said, sliding her words together lazily. It gave the older woman the air of a sophisticated nineteenth-century madame fanning herself in a fancy parlor.

Or maybe that was just Gemma's overactive imagination.

She set her tray on the bar counter, rolling her head to work the kinks out of her neck, feeling the night's humidity cling to her chest like a veil of moisture. "This does seem more like a local watering joint, but that's the fun in a place like this—getting to know the customers."

And picking their brains about Theroux. Not that she'd found out much tonight. When she'd had time to ease any questions into a conversation, the answers had been limited to, "Damien's not much for socializin' with the likes of his neighbors anymore," or, "Damien's done right by himself."

Soon, she'd talk to Roxy and the other staff. Maybe they would shed some light on the man. And as for the prostitution angle? Well, there hadn't been much traffic up and down the stairs tonight. Just a short, muscled African-American man and a woman dressed in what could only be called Irish-lass-fetish garb who'd gone up about a half hour ago.

She'd have to explore to see what was going on.

Roxy placed a pale, vein-etched hand on Gemma's arm, squeezing it. "You done well tonight, Gem. I checked on those references you left, and I'm hoping you're one to stick around this place."

Good. Gemma had asked some California friends to pretend that they were ex-employers who'd hired Gem James. They'd obviously come through for her.

Roxy added, "I still need that paperwork, though."

"I'll get it to you." She was procuring some false documentation, complete with a fake Garden District address, that would be ready tomorrow.

Patrons were starting to leave the bar, slowing the night's pace. Gemma sighed and slipped a hand to the back of her bared neck, kneading her nape.

"How about you go into the back room and get me some napkins?" Roxy asked. "And take a few minutes off those feet while you're there."

"Thanks." Gemma thought about staying to talk with the waitress for a second, but decided instead to seek privacy and scribble down some notes. There would be time to gab with Roxy and the other workers later.

After winking at the string-bean bartender, Wedge, who pointed his finger like a gun at her and winked back, Gemma entered a room stacked with cardboard supply boxes and bottles of liquor. She found her purse where she'd tucked it on a shelf between two pillars of paper napkins, then attacked her notepad with gusto.

She scribbled colorful details about the bar and the customers for about ten minutes, realizing how little she'd turned up so far.

Back at the office, she'd done some preliminary research on Theroux, not finding anything she hadn't already known. Thirty-four years old, business owner, New Orleans native. Real exciting stuff. Tomorrow she would have more time to do a deeper search, but still…

She wanted more. What she had—even for day number one—wasn't nearly good enough.

Heavy footsteps sounded on the hallway tiles, and Gemma scrambled to put away her notes.

The door swung open, revealing Damien Theroux.

Her blood twisted direction, shocking her system, leaving her weak with a mix of attraction and guilt.

Whoo, he was tall. Slim, but solid enough to fill out that black suit. It wasn't hard to picture toned abs and cable-muscled arms under those fancy clothes. Unlike this afternoon, when his dark hair had been loose, he'd secured the top strands away from his face with a band, allowing the bottom to wave down to his wide shoulders.

Time to go to work again.

She forced herself to meet his blue-diamond eyes. "I'm just taking a break," she blurted.

Suave. Could her words have been any more spastic?

"Roxy says you're back here for napkins."

He leaned against the brick wall, taking his time, bracing himself with one shoulder as he ran his other hand over his angled jaw. He smoothed a gaze over her.

From her pumps…up her bare legs…over her skirt… her torso…her breasts…still on her breasts…still on her…

Gemma covered her chest with her arms, blocking him.

He smiled, doused it, then glanced up at her from beneath his dark brows. "I like your pirate motif."

The skull and crossbones. Right. "Don't you mean 'motifs'?"

"Those, too."

There they went—the *motifs*—hardening into sensitive peaks that brushed the cotton of her shirt. As she adjusted position, keeping her arms crossed and leaning nonchalantly against the shelves, her nipples scraped against the outsides of her thumbs. A flush roared over her body, prickling her skin with new sweat and heat.

"Am I disturbing you?" he asked.

She tried to stay unaffected. "You walked in the door just as I was trying to relax. Scared me half to death."

As if to prove it, she raised a hand to massage her neck again, leaving the other arm to still cover evidence of her inconvenient desire.

Theroux unfolded himself from the wall, stepped forward.

Fear shot through her, but not because she felt threatened. No, this was the safe fear of her fantasies, where unknown men would approach her, cover her with their shadows, slip into her, then disappear into the corners of her mind.

A stirring, a warm shivering, bloomed in the pit of her stomach. She slid her palm there, liking it. Hoping it would stop.

He was still moving toward her.

The rational part of her panicked. "So, do you hit on all the new waitresses, like some sort of initiation?"

Why had she said that? Because she thought it would create some kind of distance she didn't really want?

He paused a mere foot away, his taut body remaining as still as a held breath. "If you think I'm hitting on you now, *chérie,* you've got some lessons to learn."

Another blush prickled over her skin. "It's just… My space bubble. I don't think you're aware of the concept."

"Am I getting a little too close now?"

"For a stranger."

Tilting back his head, he surveyed her, a grin quirking his mouth. He had a full lower lip. Sensuous, soft.

"Stranger," he repeated, rolling the word over his tongue, savoring it.

That slightly exotic accent—a tinge of French?— stretched over her, bare and slick, burying her under its promising weight.

By now, Gemma couldn't contain the excited quiver traveling her limbs, settling between her legs with electric anticipation.

Theroux must have sensed that she liked the way he'd touched her this afternoon. That she wanted to test the dark waters outside of her wading pool. And maybe…

No.

Yes. Maybe this was a good way to ask a personal question or two. It'd worked for Mata Hari.

He moved closer to her. Closer. Inches away, until he was staring down, arm curved over her head as he rested it on the shelves, body slightly hunched, eclipsing everything else around them.

His scent filled her—rain, brandy—making her giddy.

"A stranger?" he whispered. "I'm easy to know."

While Gemma pressed her arm against her sensitized breasts again, the hand she held against her neck tightened involuntarily. "Listen, you're not my type."

"Yeah?"

He took up where they'd left off this afternoon, with him skimming his palm up her arm to capture her hand—the one rubbing her neck. The weight of his touch reduced her next words into a quiet struggle to suck in oxygen.

"I usually…go for more…of the roses and…chocolates guy."

Theroux pressed his thumb up her wrist, up the middle of her palm, finding a spot that made her want to giggle, cry and rub herself against him all at the same time. He traced circles, reducing her to helplessness.

"You get that sort of pansy boy in California, for certain," he said, watching her.

She couldn't meet his gaze, not straight on, so she glanced up at him through her eyelashes. "How do you know I'm from…?" She gasped as he gave her delicate palm nerve an especially persuasive nudge. "Ah. Oh. Right. You must've talked to Roxy about me."

Dammit, she was supposed to be questioning *him.*

"She'd have all the information, being the boss round here." With unexpected care, he lowered her hand, then slid his own around her neck, massaging her tense muscles.

"Mmm." In spite of her caution, Gemma leaned into the pressure. "And what else do you know about me?"

"Not much. Just that you follow…*strangers*…down streets and into dark bars."

"I told you, I need this job."

Theroux kept rubbing, watching. Gemma's chest rose and fell, marking the seconds.

"Let me guess what you're about," he said. "I think you're a 'never left.' One of many who came to this place just to visit. You fell in love with the jazz, the Creole sauces, the romance of not knowing what goes on behind the lace curtains. Then, as we say, you never left."

He'd gotten most of it, except the part he'd skipped about coming here with the hopes of finding a life, too.

"And you?" she asked. "Why are you in New Orleans?"

Theroux paused, then trailed his hand from her neck to her collarbone, running his fingers under her tank top's neckline until his nails smoothed against the tender skin of her upper chest. Without thinking, Gemma took her arm from her breasts, reached out to grab his jacket's lapel, leaving herself open.

Obviously encouraged, he slid his fingers outside the material of her shirt, cupping a breast, tracing his thumb over the awakened crest of it. Gemma winced, arching into his caress. Her other hand mindlessly shot out to cover his knuckles in pleased wariness.

What the hell was she doing?

"I think maybe you like strangers," he said, ignoring her personal questions.

Not that she could remember what they'd just been talking about.

Fascinated by his aggression, her fingers moved with his as he absently toyed with her nipple.

"I think," he continued in that soft, lethal whisper, "that you aren't what you seem."

Her heart punched against her ribs, then wavered in real fear. He couldn't know she was a reporter. How…?

Theroux lowered his lips to her ear, his breath warm. "You tease. You act nice. But that's not what you want, a nice man."

Thank God, he didn't know. The buzz of passing danger melted downward, coating her with dampness, readiness. She wanted him to touch her there, to give her what she *really* wanted.

"I do want a nice man," she said. "I've been looking for one, but…"

He skimmed his hand down her ribs, over the curve of her butt, the back of her thigh, searching.

"…it never seems to work out."

"I wonder why."

She did, too. She *did* like nice guys, even if they'd never been enough to hold her interest. But that was her fault, not theirs. She'd tried a few normal, home-by-six-for-dinner relationships, tried men her family approved of.

But there was something untamed in Gemma. Maybe something might be wired wrong in her. Was it normal to lust after men like Theroux? To find yourself in a position like *this?*

She reached down and captured his wandering hand with hers, putting an end to the spell.

For a moment, he froze. Without moving, he created a space between them with the sting of his gaze.

"I think my break's over," she said, voice wavering. She cleared her throat. "First night. Good impression. All that."

A calculating smile settled on his mouth. Reaching up, he grabbed a packet of napkins, deposited it into Gemma's hand, then backed away.

"Roxy'll wonder what took you so long," he said. "Should I tell her?"

He was baiting Gemma, so she sent him her toughest glance. "Your call, boss."

"As I said, Roxy's in charge. I'm inconsequential to this bar."

She'd see about that.

He ushered her away from the shelves with a sweep of his arm. "After you."

Had she alienated him with her hot/cold change of reaction? Way to go, Duncan. Gemma could almost hear Waller Smith congratulating her on messing up already.

Much more painfully, she could hear her first boss saying, *When you're assigned a story, you get your ass out there and do it. Don't piddle around. Your scaredy-cat caution has no place in this business, girl.*

She left the room, feeling her redemption—Theroux—following right behind her.

Toughen up, she thought. Next time, don't stop. Get your man, no matter the consequences.

When she emerged into the bar again, she turned around to fire a parting shot at her mysterious subject.

But he'd already disappeared.

WALLER SMITH LIKED A proper nap.

So, as he sat at the Cuffs bar, his body relaxing on the scuffed wood, Waller sighed, content.

In his forty-four years of life, he'd sat on a lot of bar stools across the country, liking how the chattery, friendly voices made him feel a part of something. In fact, even if he nursed one gin and tonic all night, he always fell asleep to the lullaby of conversations.

New York, L.A., Dallas, Miami, Chicago. He'd lived in all the big cities, getting jobs at local papers to support himself and trolling the bars for a kind voice or two. Tonight, he'd decided to try Cuffs, not only because he wanted companionship, but because it'd come highly recommended by Ms. Gemma Duncan during her unsuspecting story pitch to The General.

And speaking of the little devil, Gemma had emerged into the bar again.

See, not only could Waller sleep on a dime, he could wake up with the best of them, too. It just took a sound, a feeling. The best sleepers could all stay slightly alert in their slumber.

Screw the fact that his ex-wife had chalked up the ever-increasing number of his naps to depression. Waller merely believed he was getting older. More used up and worn out.

Fully awake now—except for some blurred vision— he watched his co-worker, the newest reporter at the *Weekly Gossip,* strolling out of a back room, tailed by none other than Damien Theroux himself.

She'd made quick time, hadn't she?

Waller wondered just how much information she'd gotten out of the guy. *How* she'd gotten it out of him.

Young pup. Reporters were always bright eyed and eager until a few years passed. Years of seeing bullet-riddled corpses at drive-by-shooting crime scenes. Years of seeing crack babies who'd been stranded by their strung-out mothers living on the street and prostituting themselves for their next fix.

Like Gemma, Waller used to love chasing a story.

That was before the stories chased him, caught him, burned themselves into his memory until nothing on earth could erase the images. Except a good sleep.

As Theroux disappeared into a patch of darkness behind Gemma, she straightened her tank top, turned around and found herself alone. After a beat, she raised her chin and extracted her order pad from a tiny apron while walking to a table of three old men. The few grizzled patrons who hadn't gone home yet watched her progress, enchanted.

The back room.

Tank top adjusting.

Waller sighed. He remembered the days when reporters had ethics, but if this girl wanted to use her body to get her ink on Theroux, he'd stay out of it. After all, this was New Orleans. Anything went.

After taking the order, she swayed to the bar in her heels. Waller tried to catch her eye.

When she saw him, he saluted with his full glass of booze. She hightailed it over, jaw clenched.

"Good evening," he said jovially.

"What the hell are you doing here?"

Waller pulled a pained expression out of his collection of reactions. "I'm having a drink, just like everyone else. What are *you* doing here?" He aimed a disapproving glare at the back room.

"Perv. It's not what you think."

"You don't want to know what I think."

"You haven't answered yet." Her voice lowered. "Are you crowding me?"

"Sweetness," he said, holding a hand over his food-stained heart, "I've got no ulterior motives. Remember, someone with no talent wouldn't have such drive."

She seemed to regret what she'd said at the office earlier. Truthfully, the words had whiplashed Waller. *He* knew he was useless, but the problem came when everyone else knew it, too. Not that he gave a crap.

"Smith." Gemma crept closer, eyes wide and Bambi-like. "Don't blow this for me. Please."

Unable to counter the clear ambition—no, it was *desperation*—in her words, Waller could only stare at his drink. In its clear depths, he saw his past swirl right by him—the hard-earned headlines, the awards he'd so proudly displayed on his desks, the divorce papers he'd burned in the flame of a dinner candle one lonely, bitter night.

He'd never expected to find himself huddled over a bar in the middle of the French Quarter by himself, beaten, mocking a young reporter because of her shining future.

Or was he here because she could still track down a good lead when he didn't have it in him anymore?

Gemma was shaking her head. "Why would you want to pull one over on me, Smith? You're already established."

"Actually, I'm at a dead end." His words tasted sour. "Isn't that what you meant to say?"

"No, I—"

"Listen. Maybe I came here to show you that going fishing for shark won't be as easy as you think. Maybe I came here to see if I could give this a go, myself."

Now that he'd said it out loud, Waller wondered if it

was true. Why else had he taken a detour from another boredom-filled night in his apartment?

"Gem," said a raised female voice from the other end of the bar. "You okay down there?"

Waller kept his gaze fixed on Gemma, almost daring her to tell him he wasn't good enough. But she didn't.

Instead, she nodded at the voice and ran a fidgety hand over her done-up hair. "I'm *so* onto you."

"Feisty," he said. "That's another excellent quality for a girl in your profession to have."

With a cautious look, she left him and proceeded to wait on a group of former cops. Their bygone career was obvious from the way they sat—still wary in their advancing age, but less arrogant than they probably had been in their heydays. They joked with Gemma, turning their chests toward her, open books.

Look at that. She was already back to questioning sources. Seeking answers about Theroux. Well, best of luck.

The waitress who'd talked to Gemma was now cleaning glasses two feet to the left of him. He could barely see her fuzzy figure out of the corner of his eye.

"What is this place?" he asked. "Mustang Ranch?"

She didn't stop her task. The tall stick-shape of a bartender floated past, also pretending Waller didn't exist.

Raising his voice, Waller repeated, "Just what is this place? Look at what you women wear around here—Band-Aid skirts and linguini tops!"

"You fool." The waitress, still a blur except for some flaming red hair that was layered down to her bare shoulders, sauntered over to him. "You're a mess, and it ain't from havin' enough of *our* booze, I tell you that."

"So, I'm naturally loaded."

She came closer, and Waller hitched in a breath. God, she was a beauty. Two gray streaks of hair framed her face—lightning in a red sky. Fine smile lines surrounded soft, whiskey-hued eyes. Her skin was pale, the color of smooth writing paper before you mark it with the scar of stories.

"A man with eyes so red should go on home to bed," she said in a mother-hen scold.

Waller blinked, donned his most charming smile. He hoped it still worked. "Tell me you're my guardian angel."

"Not likely."

The waitress leaned on the bar, showing ample bosom. Waller's vision cleared to an even greater extent.

"I deal with drunks every night of my life," she added. "Your sober imitation of one is not impressing me."

"No?" Waller's pulse actually slowed to almost nothing. Funny. He hadn't felt keen embarrassment in a while. There'd only been a numb string of days holding his life together.

"What *would* it take to impress you…?"

It was a cue for her to reveal a name. She shrugged. "Roxy St. Clair. If you want to look good to me, you change your messy shirt. Easy enough, huh?"

Waller checked out his lunch-decorated button-down. Was it that bad? "I suppose that's simple. What next?"

Roxy stood, smiled. "You walk out of here and get a good night's rest."

"I'll try." The dog in him wanted to ask her if she'd escort him home, but he knew better. "Anything else?"

"I need time to think on it." Roxy started to walk away, still looking at him. "Maybe we see tomorrow night?"

"That's a sure way to draw repeat business."

"It's my trick," she said.

"And a smart one."

She offered a careless gesture, sort of a curtsy, and joined Gemma and the ex-cops while the young reporter served them drinks. Their sudden explosion of laughter shook Waller to the core because he wasn't in on the joke.

Then again, when was he ever?

Grabbing a bowl of pretzels, Waller munched on them, content to hear Roxy laugh for the time being. It beat sitting in front of a TV that only got three channels.

An hour later, after the jukebox had been put to rest and Roxy was cleaning the empty tables, Waller tore his gaze away from her long enough to see the man himself, Damien Theroux, come down the stairs.

In a purely objective way, Waller could see why a woman would go gaga for him. He was tall, wide through the shoulders as a me-hunter-you-gatherer male should be. Lazily cocksure in the way he moved.

Some guys had all the luck.

With the confidence of a gambler who held a winning hand, Theroux gave a slight nod to Roxy and walked out the door. Not long afterward, Gemma wandered over to the older waitress, exchanged a few words with her and glanced toward the stairway.

Good gravy, the kid was going snooping. Her eagerness would blow this story right away. But, hell, she'd learn from her mistakes.

As Roxy went into the back room, the young reporter crept toward the steps, folding her hands together as she caught Waller's eye and sending him a pleading look that clearly said, "Shhhhh?"

Then she made her way to the second floor.

Not that Waller gave a crap about what she did. He just shrugged and went back to waiting for Roxy St. Clair to smile at him again.

4

I T WAS OBVIOUS, GEMMA thought as a stair creaked
under her high heel, that Waller Smith thought she was
crazy for coming upstairs so soon.

His jaded, be-my-guest glance had told her as much
after she'd made sure Roxy was occupied, then sneaked
up to the second floor.

Really, all Gemma wanted to do was take a quick
look around, to see if that man and woman who'd
climbed the stairs earlier in the night were still engaged
in business. To see if anyone else could've been lured
upstairs for...what? Sex? Drugs?

Damien Theroux's "other matters" that Lamont had
mentioned just this afternoon?

Discovering Smith in the bar tonight had given
Gemma a swift kick in the rear. Clearly, the older reporter was interested in Theroux's story, too. That
meant she was *really* against the clock because not only
did she have to impress her editor with some earth-
shattering information about Theroux within two
weeks, but now a co-worker was threatening to scoop
her.

And she'd be damned if that happened again.

Besides, Roxy said that Theroux had left for the night, so Gemma had a few minutes to poke around before the head waitress wondered what her new employee was up to. Since most of the patrons had gone home, too, Roxy was busy taking liquor inventory, buying Gemma some time.

Another stair protested as she put her weight on it. Gemma closed her eyes, stood still, listening to see if she'd attracted any attention.

Nothing. All she heard was an animalistic cry from somewhere down the hallway.

Yup, they were still up here—that horny couple.

Heart pumping, pulse beating in her ears, Gemma quietly climbed to the top of the landing. The hallway was dark, lit only by a flickering lantern encased by a copper-and-glass box and attached to a plank wall. The striking mélange of old wood, mustiness and sweet cigar smoke accompanied the rusty *yawp* of the floorboards as she walked over them. Several closed doors greeted her, but one had been left ajar, a thick, buttery light melting through the cracks.

Naturally, she headed toward that one, pushed it open just enough to look inside. As she did so, a cataclysmic thump from down the hall shook the wooden floor. Laughter followed.

Gemma's hyperimagination provided a reason for the crash: two bodies falling out of a bed during the throes of sex.

Gemma talked herself down. She wasn't going to get caught nosing around up here, and prizewinning reporters never let a little fear stop them.

Or even a little guilt.

So she forged ahead into the lit room, ignoring the loud giggling of her hidden, rollicking neighbors.

A Tiffany lamp offered quiet light to this... Was it an office? Damien's workplace?

Excellent. Sometimes a man's cave could tell you a lot about the guy himself.

An Asian-detailed carpet pooled under an antique cherrywood desk. A laptop computer with a laser printer contrasted sharply with the elegance of bronze sculptures, a French Empire couch, potted palms and red-hued paintings of a sleeping woman.

The good life, Gemma thought. That's what Damien Theroux was all about. Riches, decadence, excess.

Pleasure.

Spellbound, she started toward his desk, her reporter's instinct telling her to open some drawers, go through paperwork, search for something that would give her a story. At the same time, she hesitated to go through a person's belongings, souvenirs of privacy.

Then she heard it—a creak on the stairwell.

Hadn't Roxy told her that Theroux had gone home?

Darting out of the office, she shut the door to a slit, trying to leave it the way she'd found it. Then she stepped into the hall, seeking a hiding place, glancing around at all the closed rooms.

She tried one knob. Locked.

Dammit!

Then another. Locked again.

As she tried to find a deep shadow that would make for a decent cover, she perked up her ears.

Only to hear nothing more than a long, satiated female groan from the occupied room.

Great, Gemma, she thought, almost laughing at herself. You're hearing things. Theroux is safe and snug at home, and here you are, thinking he's dogging you.

Nonetheless, she didn't move for a few minutes, just in case he was walking up the steps really, *really* slowly.

While she waited, the woman's moans became rhythmic, and there was a muted thumping against the wall, as if the man had her body pinned to it, ramming into her, making her dig her nails into his back with the force of his thrusts.

Gemma leaned against her own wall, images coating her mind, dripping down her body like sweat—or the light path of a man's fingertip.

She remembered Theroux standing near the supply room doorway, watching her until she couldn't take in air. Remembered him hovering over her, his breath moistening the side of her neck. Remembered his fingers cupping her breast, molding it like an artist skimming over his work.

Caught up in the moment, Gemma slid her hand up her ribs, under her breast, separating her fingers and catching her nipple between them. Rubbing, she felt it harden under her tank and lace bra, felt it throb with yearning.

She closed her eyes, dizzy, moving her fingers in time to the drumbeat of a body thudding against old wood.

Behind the door.

"Don't tease." It was a female voice, urgent, threaded with need. "Touch me there."

Gemma's other hand glided over her belly, wishing Theroux's hand had nestled there tonight. There…and slightly below. She eased her fingers upward, under the bottom of her tank top, over her sweat-misted skin.

Did Theroux bring women up here, too? Had he made love to them in an antique bed, slipping down their bodies, parting their legs, seducing them with slow, heat-slick kisses?

Pressure, the beat of moisture, twisted between Gemma's legs. Again, she drew her hand lower.

At the same time, the woman cried out again, almost as if she were being tortured, pained with pleasure. Woven between her gasps were the low laughs of a man—the one who was making her so crazy.

What was he doing to drive her nuts?

Somewhere in the back of Gemma's mind, her inner reporter was still at large, asking questions: Was she hearing a cathouse in action? Was this only one way Damien Theroux made his money?

She wouldn't put it past a guy with his reputation.

Not that she was much better, sitting here in a red-light-playground hallway with her hand halfway to her…

Someone was pounding on the wall with a fist now, as if begging for mercy. It must have been the woman, judging by the mewling *oh-oh-oh-oh*s Gemma was hearing.

Realizing how inappropriate this was, she stood from her slouch, dropped her hand from her breast and reddened in embarrassment.

"You taking another break?" said a soft, low voice by the top of the stairway.

Scared out of her skin, Gemma jumped, knocking against the wall, hand over her heart. It flapped like a ripped flag in a storm.

She glanced up to find him—Theroux—leaning with one shoulder against the wall, the black of his tousled hair and expensive suit fading into the hall's near darkness. Only the stuttering lantern light showed her that he wore a lazy grin.

"Where did you come from?" she asked. Thing was, she knew it was the dumbest five words ever to be cobbled together, but it was a time killer. A dance around her real question.

You didn't see me getting off to this hallelujah boink-a-thon chorus, did you?

"I work here," he said, the gleam in his pale eyes letting her know that he had indeed seen her. "Remember?"

Er…yeah. She'd been remembering a lot of things, what with one hand on her boob and the other just ready to make the dive into her skirt.

What was happening to Gemma Duncan? When had she become a sexual maniac? Were rampant junior-high hormones finally kicking into gear with the help of Theroux's bad-boy stimulus?

About time.

"You know," she said, trying to fly ever so casually, "when the crowd started to leave, someone turned off the jukebox downstairs and I heard noise on this second floor. So I came up."

"To investigate?"

She nodded a little too enthusiastically.

"Brave girl." Theroux sauntered next to her, adjusted

the wavering lantern on the wall—the one she must have upset during her too-recent imitation of a rocket ship. He gestured toward her empty hands. "Next time you hear some noises, you might take care to bring a weapon or two."

Lie, Gemma, lie. "No need. I'm a black belt in…" What was it called? "…Tai-rate." Yeah. "Not to worry. I can defend myself."

"I'll be careful around you, then."

She opened her mouth to tell him that he was damned straight about that, but was interrupted by a stupendously endless moan from the room.

Gemma shot him the best clueless glance she could muster. *Whatever could that have been?*

"I think," he said, "Roxy has hired herself an audio voyeur. Is that what you are, Gem?"

Gazing at the room once again, then back at him, Gemma did her best to seem offended. "Are you calling me a Peeping—Listening Tom?"

He took another step closer, and the hallway suddenly seemed to shrink, making him the only lung-sealing focus.

"Gem," he murmured. From him, her name sounded like a fine, smooth cognac. Able to drive a man to dream, to soothe him into ecstasy.

She'd never heard any guy say her name that way before. Maybe it was because she'd always been "Gemma," not some undercover slut waitress who couldn't control herself in the steam of New Orleans.

But why should she be ashamed about that? She was up here—staking the place out, listening through the door to a lovemaking session—because this was her job.

And because the sounds had struck an erotic chord in her.

He glanced down at her skirt. "Put your hands back where they were."

She offered a shaky, disbelieving laugh, a buzz of carnal curiosity traveling deep inside her, riding her nerves, kissing her skin.

He knew that Gemma wanted to be touched, to feel what that woman was feeling behind the closed door.

And who but her and Theroux would ever know?

Who would care after her story was finished?

The anonymous man in the room started to murmur in French, strained endearments to the tune of the woman's gasps.

Theroux leaned over, his breath tickling Gemma's ear as she avoided looking at him. "What do you feel right now?"

"Mortification." And the wish to be left alone, where she could've let loose and enjoyed herself in the dark of her own apartment. No one would see her there. No one would watch as she laid herself bare, vulnerable, opening everything she kept undercover in public.

Another naked groan from the room.

"You're flushed," he said. "Beautiful. What if I were to make you cry out like that, *chérie?* Has a man ever made you come so hard?"

His bold words jarred her, excited her, made her realize that, no, Gemma Duncan had never been rocked like a hurricane in her life.

"Don't talk to me like you know me," she said, trying to stay afloat, in control of herself. "You don't. Not at all."

"I don't?" He laughed softly. "Certainly I know when a woman wants to be touched. What's your favorite spot, Gem? A long kiss behind the knee? A finger tracing up your spine?" He sketched his mouth over her ear. "A hard whisper against your clit?"

The couple inside the room had resumed their wall-thumping marathon, but now a man's *ah*s had been added. His voice mingled with hers, keeping time to the tempo of body hitting wood.

Gemma ached, literally hurting because of the burn, the throb, of her sex. Pride was keeping her from touching herself, from making herself feel better.

Because once she stepped over this line with Theroux, there was no going back.

Then again, why was the idea of being plain old, boring Gemma so appealing, anyway? Right now, that's the last thing she wanted—to stay safe. To stay in a dull, unchallenging flat of existence.

Even as she fell further into temptation, the inner reporter couldn't help making one last-ditch attempt at self-preservation.

"What kind of business are you running, Mr. Theroux?" She could barely get the words out, what with him so close.

With her body balanced on this live wire.

"Shhhh," he said, turning her away from him and covering her mouth with a hand. Callused skin rubbed against her lips, and she could smell a memory of liquor on his fingers.

She closed her eyes, lost, pressing her hand over her stomach.

"You ask too many questions," he said.

Gemma tried to ask another one, but he tightened his hold on her—not enough to hurt, but enough to get his point across.

DAMIEN DIDN'T WANT to talk about business. He wanted to forget about it, just for a night.

Besides, she could assume what she wanted about him, this woman who got turned on by naughty games. The Gems of the world were perfect for Damien—quick and easy, leaving him to pursue his own life in the mornings. He'd never experienced anything more than this type of relationship in his life. He'd known it was for the best, ever since he'd started to like girls way back when.

A round of frenzied swearing sounded from behind the closed door.

Kumbar and his longtime lady friend. The only time they got to see each other anymore was after hours, when her waitressing shift at the Irish pub down the street ended and when he finished with Club Lotus business. Damien didn't mind them using the rooms by his office so much. They were always empty, anyway.

Though Gem had gone still, her heart beat double time against Damien's arm. Lust speared through him at the thought of what might be running through her mind, her body.

He knew she was on the edge.

"You like what you hear?" he whispered into her ear. "Is that why you were…?"

He felt, more than heard, her surrendering moan. It

echoed over the skin of his palm, electrifying his nerve endings.

When he'd come up the stairs to find her in such a suggestive pose, Damien had stopped in his tracks, unable to move. Watching the way she'd shyly tested her body had transfixed him. Turned him on so he was likely to explode.

Playing with her in the supply room earlier hadn't satisfied him at all. He needed so much more.

"Please!" said Kumbar's girl, voice muffled. "Oh, please…"

As Gem breathed against his palm, she leaned her head back against his shoulder, coasting her hand farther down her belly.

Aw, damn, she was doing it. A rush of blood consumed his cock, heating it.

"What's going on in that room, Gem?" he said, encouraging her while trying to keep his voice even, unaffected.

She raised one arm, grabbed his shoulder for purchase, then sketched her hand between her legs, rubbing. He watched her slow strokes, the tiny gyrations of her hips.

Kumbar was starting to make Kandi scream.

Now, Damien took his hand from Gem's mouth, wanting to hear the quickening of her breath, the little *um* sounds she was making as she kept her face turned away from him.

What he'd give to touch her, too. To put his hand over hers and work her to a puddle. To undo his zipper, part her legs and ease into her.

But something told him to hold back—to watch and enjoy.

And he did, over and over again.

As Kumbar and Kandi came down the home stretch, Gem arched away from Damien, her body slumping as her legs gave way. He held her up, liking the feel of keeping her next to his chest, just this once.

Moments passed while she panted and grabbed his arm to stay upright. In an unexplainable move, he traced a stray damp piece of blond hair off her cheek, tucked it behind her ear.

She felt so soft. Smelled nice, too, like lemons.

But then he realized what he was doing, and he built his flood walls back up. Kept the tide of emotion from flowing over him, just as the barriers erected along the banks of the Big River did.

Keeping the damage away.

He whispered to her once again. "So tell me—why were you creeping around up here?"

She stiffened, and he could almost hear an answer being created in her mind.

Then, pushing at his arms and struggling to stand as she stumbled away, Gem faced him.

The wild red of her cheeks and the blaze of her blue eyes goaded him to forget that she was on the second floor, where she didn't belong. All he wanted to do right now was take her by the hand and lead her to a waiting bed somewhere, in a place where he could shed his responsibilities for a night.

"I told you why," she said, and he could see that she was piecing together her dignity. That maybe she was even the type of woman who didn't orgasm in hallways with men they'd known for less than a day.

"If you intend to keep your job," he said, going back to his lackadaisical, good-old-boy act, "don't come up here again. As you found, there's nothing but trouble on the second floor."

Kumbar's room had gone quiet, leaving them with little to say. And that was all for the good. Damien didn't feel like commenting on the sudden panicked hurt in her gaze. The Red-Riding-Hood-in-the-woods look.

She folded her arms over her breasts, glanced at the floor. "I won't go exploring again. I'll stick downstairs, though I'm not sure it's entirely safe down there, either."

The supply room. Ah, yes.

And with that, she walked away, never even looking at him, leaving Damien frustrated and still aching for a good time.

In an attempt to cool off, he waited in his office, giving Kumbar and his woman enough time to get it together before barging in. When Damien had left Cuffs earlier to go for a little walk around the neighborhood, he'd only been waiting to talk to his right-hand guy. Damien respected the fact that everyone needed time for a nice, old-fashioned hump. Sex cleared the mind.

At least, that was usually the theory.

Fifteen minutes later, the door squealed open and Kandi came flitting out, dressed in her green corset-and-skirt waitress garb. Her curly black hair flared out in bed-head disarray as she burst into Theroux's office.

"Working too hard, my man?"

"'Night, Kandi."

"*Oph,* the fellow means business." She waved on her way out. "I'll leave you alone, then, crabby cakes."

And she was off, leaving Kumbar to take her place. From the patient way the buff, dark man propped his fists on his hips, Damien knew Kumbar had read his boss's restlessness. He was ready to receive some orders.

"My sixth sense is prickling," Damien said, leaning back in his leather chair and glancing out the window at the nighttime malaise of Burgundy Street, with its run-down houses and corner grocery.

Kumbar just waited.

"Do me a favor, would you?" Damien said. "Look into our new waitress. See to her story. Gem James from California. Roxy should have more information. Got that?"

After nodding, Kumbar tilted his head toward the door.

"Yeah, go back to it now." Damien waved away his employee, then continued to stare out the window.

Wondering where Gem James went when the night was done.

GEMMA COULD BARELY KEEP her eyes open the next afternoon as she tailed another subject out of a strip joint on Bourbon Street.

A seventy-three-year-old burlesque legend, the topic of her next local-color tale for the tabloids.

Working two jobs was going to be pure hell, thought Gemma. But if that's what it took to get the story of a lifetime, she'd sure do it. That, and more.

A twinge of discomfort pinched at her as she trailed Delia Sherbert past the day-quiet tourist bars, with their daiquiris and pizzas. Past the peep shows and the festive masks peeking out of the souvenir stores.

Boy, for a woman who should be at home knitting baby booties for her grandkids, Delia Sherbert was in phenomenal shape.

Yes, that's right, Gemma thought. Keep thinking of the old woman's daily workouts and frequent plastic surgery. Keep your mind off last night, by all means.

What had she been thinking? She'd entirely lost her head when Theroux had even gotten near her.

Heat flared over her skin as she recalled his effect on her. Stoking her inner temperature. Bringing her to a climax. Oh, man. She—Gemma Duncan, class valedictorian—had reached the big *O* while listening to another couple having sex.

How warped was she?

Still, she couldn't help smiling. It was kind of fun, kind of interesting, seeing what she had in her. Exploring these new territories was actually exciting.

But she wouldn't let it go further than it had last night, when she'd made her decision to give into a little pleasure.

Next time she saw Theroux, she'd act like she masturbated in front of men every day of the week. No biggie. He was nothing special. She'd do it for anyone, right?

After she sidestepped a questionable puddle near a gutter—damned frat boys—Gemma caught her subject rounding the corner of St. Peter, where she eventually stopped at a Jackson Square hot-dog cart to grab lunch.

Putting on her politest face, Gemma approached Delia Sherbert, introducing herself and offering to buy her a meal. No stranger to publicity, the woman heard Gemma out, and even agreed to sit on the stone steps near the Cabildo and chat. There, while they blended into a crowd of tourists and bohemian/homeless types—Gemma couldn't tell which—she took out her minirecorder and notepad. Then, she listened as Delia responded to persistent rumors that she was pregnant—uh, yeah, *pregnant*—by the twenty-year-old son of a local politician.

As Delia embraced the speculation, making Gemma wonder if the old woman had started the wacky story herself, a shiver ran down the reporter's back. As if she was being watched.

When she looked around, she found an intimidating man moving through the square with a shorter guy who had spiked brown hair.

The taller one was Damien Theroux.

Out of instinct, she held up her notepad to shield her face, even though he was passing right by, acting as if he hadn't seen her at all.

What was up with her reporter radar? Last night, when Theroux had sneaked up on her in the hallway, she hadn't sensed a thing. Now, when he didn't even seem to know she was around, her nerves were screaming.

"You all right, honey?" Delia asked, reaching out a talon-tipped hand to pat Gemma's shoulder.

"Oh. Sure. It's the sun." Gemma pointed toward the sky, where light was indeed beaming down upon them. More often than not, she realized how much she'd come to depend on lying to get by in her job. She wasn't sure if she liked that or not.

"We'll have to get you some Delia Sherbert sunglasses," the woman said, gesturing to the monstrosities on her heavily made-up face. Her blue lenses were edged by poodles and clouds. "They're for sale at Delia's burlesque joint."

"I'll buy some on the way back." And Gemma would, if only to increase the peace among journalists and prey in the city. "If everyone looked like Delia Sherbert, I'd have to say the world would be a better place."

She was getting *so* good at kissing up, too.

"Girl," the stripper said, patting cherry-red hair that was sprayed to within an inch of its life, "Delia likes the way you think." She polished off the rest of her hot dog. "What you say to coming back to the shop? Delia will show you around some and give you everything you need for that article of yours. Delia don't answer phones, so you'd best get what you can while Delia's available."

Gemma already knew that Delia didn't answer phones. That was why she'd had to hunt her down. "Let's go, then, Ms. Sherbert."

"Delia. It's the professional name."

And as Gemma continued her day job, she couldn't help but look forward to the intrigue of her night one.

Where she'd use her *own* professional name.

5

DAMIEN HAD SEEN HIS WAITRESS in Jackson Square, all right. But what had she been doing hanging around with the Quarter's most famous diva? And why had Gem been writing on a notepad?

He didn't want to think what he was thinking.

"Dam," Jean said, waving a hand in front of his childhood friend's face. "What're you looking glum for?"

"Nothing that can't be fixed by a good meal."

They were sitting in one of Damien's favorite joints, Rita's. Locals could tell you that this was the first African-American-owned restaurant in the Quarter. That, with its Billie Holiday paintings, green-feather-boa ceiling trim and white plaster which offered peeks of artfully displayed brick, patrons didn't come for the view. That it served Creole and Cajun meals that made a fellow sit back with his arm over the chair and his hand on his belly while the ceiling fans whipped at the humidity.

As a matter of fact, both Damien and Jean were dining on the excellent *étoufée*, with its small, tender shrimp napping on a bed of rice and covered with a lightly spiced, tomato-tinged sauce. By the end of this very late lunch, after the bananas Foster, both men would feel as if life couldn't get any better.

The food's comfort never failed Damien, even if the other people in his life did.

Jean was waiting his friend out, probably knowing that Damien would spill his concerns somewhere between the next beer and the last bite of the main course. And he did.

"It's hard to find good help these days," Damien said.

"That's no lie."

Tourists walked by the open full-length window next to their table, heads in maps, trying to find their way down St. Philip. Damien carelessly watched them.

"Take my new waitress," he said. "I don't understand her. Not at all. Saw her jawing with Delia Sherbert by the cathedral. Didn't think she was the type to get cozy with an enterprising stripper."

The sound of Jean putting his drinking glass on the table made Damien turn back to him. His friend's dark brown eyes—*charmer's eyes,* he'd always called them, because they were surrounded by thick lashes the women loved—flashed with curiosity.

"What type did you think she was?" Jean asked.

"Didn't stop to consider." Damien went back to surveying the street.

"Well, I'll be."

He turned back to Jean. "What?"

"You." Jean leaned on his elbows, smiling and exposing a gap between his front teeth. "You're talking about a girl, Dam."

Catching the other man's meaning, Damien concentrated on sopping the last of the sauce off his plate with a thick slice of bread. "I ain't *talking* about her."

"You've gone and gotten interested in some waitress at your bar. When did this happen?"

"I hired someone yesterday, but…"

"Ah, the blush of first love. I knew it'd come around and find you one day."

Love. Damien wanted to laugh. "It ain't nothing but a passing itch."

"And you've scratched plenty enough to know."

Jean sat back in his seat while their waiter, the gallant George, prepared a tableside cooking station for their dessert. For bananas Foster, George would combine the cinnamon-coated bananas, a big, fat pat of butter, a cup of brown sugar plus rum and crème de banana right there, flames and all. The result would be a thick sauce to be drizzled over creamy vanilla ice cream.

"By the way," Jean added, "how's Mrs. Murphy?"

Damien searched his mind for the name. Ah, yeah. The wife of a former gaming mark. A woman he'd seduced last week, just to top injury with insult to her husband.

And why not? The man had headed a fraudulent charity, bilking too many trusting people out of their good money. But they'd gotten it back, thanks to Club Lotus.

"Don't be cute about my proclivities, Jean."

"Just asking. Just pointing out how unlike you it is to be actually interested in a girl."

George arrived and started his culinary magic, so Damien stayed silent for the moment.

He didn't want to talk about his personal life here. It was all business, anyway. *Sex* was just another word for *power.* Sex was another way to make him stronger.

So why had he felt a spark of something else for Gem last night? Why had he grown some kind of soft spot that had convinced him to push aside her hair, to feel a gentle need for more?

Because it'd been a long night, that's why. Nothing else.

When they had their desserts in front of them, Jean decided to make Damien even more uncomfortable.

"My dad's asking about you. He's got a concerned eye on his favorite almost-son, too."

Mr. Dulac had taken a paternal liking to Damien ever since *Papa* had passed away. Even though he didn't need watching over, Damien was still grateful.

After devouring a heap of ice cream and sauce, Jean continued. "When's this all going to stop, Dam? He wants to know. *I* want to know."

"It'll stop when I run out of bastards to fleece."

Jean carefully put down his spoon, eyebrows knitted. But Damien cut him off before another scolding came his way.

"If every conversation from now on becomes a lecture, Jean, I'll tell you now—I understand why. But no matter how much your papa or you protest, I'll keep doing my work. I know how much your daddy invested in me, and I know I'd be nothing without his help, but I'm running my own place. Leave the subject be."

They finished their meal in silence, but his friend had planted guilt in Damien. Not that he'd ever been far from it.

He wondered what *Papa* would say about his life now: how he'd started out a kid from the poor section of town, then met Jean when they were both ten, while hanging outside of a bar shooting dice with other boys. From there, Damien had almost become a part of the Dulac family—Armand, Jean's father, had allowed Damien to shuttle money from his gaming establishments to the laundering facilities. Then, he'd put Damien in charge of one bar, two bars, three. After that, when Damien had acquired his own nest egg, he'd started buying his own businesses with Armand's backing—including Club Lotus.

Years later, he was debt-free, at least monetarily.

After lunch, when they both were leaning their arms on the backs of their seats and resting their hands on their contented stomachs, Damien got a phone call from Kumbar.

As he listened to what his security pro had to tell him about Gem James, he gripped the tablecloth. It got to the point where Jean had to grab the linen on his side to prevent dishes from clattering to the floor.

"Thank you," Damien said to Kumbar. "You've done well."

And he closed his cell phone.

"I'm not even going to ask," Jean said.

Great, now that Damien needed to let off some steam. He went full blast ahead, anyway, trying to hold in the rage, the sear of betrayal.

"That waitress?" he said. "She's got some explaining to do."

"Go on."

George brought the bill, and Damien beat Jean in reaching into his pants pocket first to take care of it. On his way to his wallet, he felt the two cards he always carried—his morning blackjack shuffle.

A ten of clubs and a six of diamonds. A hand that could've been much better.

"It seems," Damien said, "my new employee is a tabloid reporter. Gemma Duncan of the *Weekly Gossip*."

"Ah, what a mess."

The anger slapped at him again, but Damien took it in hand, freezing himself into control.

He merely smiled.

Jean could obviously read the gesture for what it was—pissed. "What, Dam?"

"Tell me, what keeps someone in my business alive in this town?"

"A reputation."

"A fellow doesn't need guns as much as the thought of them, sometimes. You think a tabloid reporter can manage to make me look worse than it appears right now?"

"I don't know, you being such an angel and all." Jean was narrowing his eyes, on the same page as Damien. "A man's reputation can make competitors think twice about crossing him."

"And depending on what a reporter hears about a man, he can make himself quite a son of a bitch, can't he?"

"Are you thinking about feeding her lies just to keep the competition in check?"

"She's on my tail for a story, yeah? Why not give her one and help my cause at the same time? This way, La-mont and his type won't have ammunition, because *I'll* already have gone to the press. I'll make any attack on my character useless by attacking myself first."

"This is a risky game."

"What is life without some risk?" Damien leaned back in his chair again, relaxing, taking the heat of the afternoon in stride.

That's right, he thought, watching as his friend shook his head and moved up to the next level of worrying about him. Gem James—or Gemma Duncan—would get her story.

His very own badass version of it.

LATER, IN A CORPORATE kitchen in the *Weekly Gossip*'s office on the other side of Canal Street, Gemma Duncan walked around Waller Smith, who was napping on a table surrounded by some kind of liquid-diet lunch.

Fascinating. Now his shirts would be strawberry-shake-pink instead of gumbo-beige.

Nancy Mendoza was taking a late-day break by the refrigerator, too. She handed her employee a diet cola and whispered, "Haven't seen you all day. How're things?"

"Great." Gemma shot a glance at Smith and his slumber-limp lips, then decided he was truly asleep. She'd kept mum about his possible pursuit of the story because she knew she could beat him to the news flash. There wasn't any doubt in her mind about it.

Pretty much.

Continuing with her newly found semiconfidence, Gemma updated Nancy on Delia Sherbert and how the editor would have the story by deadline, no problem.

"And what about…?" Nancy mouthed the name *Theroux*.

"Yes…there is *that*."

Besides interviewing Delia, Gemma had gotten in touch with a *Times-Picayune* crime-beat reporter, seeking more information about Damien Theroux. As expected, the "legit" journalist had sniffed at her *Weekly Gossip* credentials and offered little to no enlightenment.

Instead, Gemma had done a complete database search, gathering information about Theroux's connections with the local mob. Not bad. It gave her some leads. She'd also gotten in touch with Jerome Lamont, the man who'd been begging Theroux in the courtyard yesterday. He'd refused to talk with her, but she'd detected fear in his voice.

Would Theroux sic the mob on him if he talked? She'd have to work on convincing Lamont to come clean with her.

When Gemma ended her update, Nancy was fixing those intelligent brown eyes on her, as if she was digging deeper.

"You were wondering…?" Gemma asked.

"What else is going on in your head," Nancy finished. She'd jammed a pencil through her bun today, making her seem extra scholarly. "You're blushing like someone's bottom after a good spank."

Still in the mood after last night, Gemma considered the activity.

"What going on?" her friend asked.

Once again, Gemma peeked at Smith, then huddled with Nancy in an all-girl conspiracy by the sink.

"I'm talking to you as a buddy right now, not your reporter, okay?"

Nancy donned a gossip-loving smile. No wonder she did a bang-up job running a tabloid.

Gemma continued. "Damien Theroux is kinda hot."

"Oh, no. As your editor, I'm telling you—"

"Take off the chief hat, please? I need chick talk right now."

"I'm going to regret this, but—" she assumed chatterbox mode again "—tell me all."

It'd been so long since Gemma had been halfway excited about a man that she wasn't sure how to start.

"Don't leave me hanging," Nancy said.

"All right. Have you ever dated a guy who persuades you to do things you'd never, ever, do in real life? I'm talking about dropping your inhibitions, getting a little wild, that sort of thing."

With a faraway gleam to her gaze, Nancy sighed. "Oh, yeah. Once. Just out of college. There was this whole leather phase I went through…."

She shot a glance toward Smith, who was still breathing evenly. Even though they were whispering, the content of their conversation seemed to amplify the words.

"That's what I'm talking about," Gemma said softly. "Um, not the leather part, but the spirit of what you're saying. I've always wondered what it'd be like to look into darkness."

"Remember—the darkness looks back into you." Even as she was saying it, Nancy seemed wistful.

"That's the thrill." Gemma held the sweating cola

can against her cheek, trying to cool herself down, even in air-conditioning. "There are guys who make you wonder if you've been playing by the right rules your whole life. If you should maybe start another game, just to see how you'll do, if you'll like it."

"You're scaring me, Gemma."

"Oh, don't worry. I'm just—" she shrugged "—lusting a little. Theroux just does something to my gimme-some-naughty hormones."

Nancy the editor was starting to emerge again. Gemma could tell by the way the woman was screwing up her mouth in doubt. Maybe this was a conversation best reserved for piña coladas and nachos *after* her story was written.

"I'm being very careful," Gemma said.

Careful to retain control. Careful to keep her humanity in the face of ruining another person.

Nancy still didn't seem convinced. "Keep me posted? And don't do anything unprofessional. I mean it."

"Yes, boss." Gemma sent her a confident grin. "I've got it all locked up."

Somewhere, the gods were laughing.

In short order, Nancy returned to her office and Gemma leaned against the counter, finishing her drink, catching a rest before she hung up her "freaks and geeks" gig and went to her real job—investigating Theroux.

"Give it up," said a slurred voice from the center of the room.

Gemma tipped her can to the awakening Waller

Smith and tried not to think about how much he'd just heard from the big, whispering mouths of her and Nancy. "Was last night's attempt to scoop my story too much for you?"

Arms stretched over his head, the older reporter looked around the room as if he didn't quite know where he was. Then he recovered, blinking at her and smiling.

"Negative, Duncan. As a matter of fact, I feel very refreshed, just like I could go to Cuffs again and take in some local color."

"I told you—stay away."

He tapped the Formica tabletop with his fingers. *Thu-ronk. Thu-ronk.*

"Normally," he said, "I would. I'm just in this office for the alien-baby articles and the paycheck. Isn't that what everyone says about me?"

So he wasn't deaf to popular opinion, after all. Gemma wondered what kind of man would take the backbiting, would seem not to give a fig about it.

Suddenly, she wondered about Smith's life. Did he have one?

"I'm curious," she said, walking closer to his table. "How did you come to work at this paper if you hate it?"

His bleary eyes registered surprise, as if he thought no one would've ever cared to ask. Then, he covered up the lapse with a yawn. "I guess being on staff here is my reward for being such a hard worker all my life."

Sure.

"But," he continued, "I feel the old me returning. Yes, siree, the old Smith is back."

"Okay, I'm dying to ask. What's the old Smith like compared to the new one? Did he sleep as much? And why this change of attitude?"

"Hey, one man's slumber is another man's meditation. I do my best thinking when I snore."

He got up from the table, and Gemma noticed that he had on a clean shirt. Wrinkled, but spotless.

With attention to detail, he cleaned up his sack lunch. "I've got a fire lit under me, Duncan. It just takes one epiphany to do that to a person."

"An epi—" She tried to gauge just when he'd transformed.

When he turned around from dumping his lunch in the trash, he had a corny glow on his face.

"Oh, my god," she said. "Are you in love or something?"

"Love, schmove. All I know is that I'm going back to Cuffs tonight." He wiggled his eyebrows at her and left the room.

She'd keep her eye on him. Smith was a seasoned reporter, and Gemma wouldn't underestimate his skills.

As far as she was concerned, the battle lines had been drawn.

WHEN WALLER GOT TO CUFFS that night, he was running on all cylinders.

Especially when he spotted Roxy across the room, her red hair glowing under an overhead lamp as she served beers to some old men in suspenders playing pool.

She was wearing a silky black tank top, jiggling ever

so slightly when she walked. A formfitting skirt. Heels, which showed off her slender calves to great advantage. The silver strands of her hair framed her face like a halo, and it made Waller go a bit goofy in the head.

Gemma showed up behind the bar, blocking his view while madly wiping down a glass with a towel. She was wearing her own version of the dark-bar uniform— short skirt and a tank with the words *Sugar Me Sweet* spelled out with rhinestones.

"Get. Out," she said.

"Just giving you all some business." Waller gestured around the near-empty room. It was still early, and he knew it would get more crowded. At that point, competing with all the other customers for Roxy's attention would be much tougher.

He must've gone back to staring at the redhead like a pup, because suddenly Gemma was tapping his arm with an index finger.

"Are you…?" She jerked her head toward the head waitress, widened her eyes.

"What if I am?"

"Is that why you're here? Because you've got it bad for Roxy? Poor woman."

Waller jerked back. Had he become that disgusting to females once he'd crossed over into the badlands of forty?

"I didn't mean it that way," Gemma said, indeed looking sorry. A little. As much as a brash young whippersnapper like her could, anyway.

"Get me a gin and tonic and let me do my work," he grumped, his ego having been smacked into reality.

"I don't think so." Gemma set down the glass and

planted her hands on the bar, seeming very territorial while shooting him a glare. "Get your own…"

Her words came to a skidding slide.

Behind him, Waller could feel that someone had entered the room. Maybe it was the rush of air. Maybe it was the reporter's eyes in the back of his skull.

But whoever it was, he had Gemma's full attention.

Waller just laughed to himself, remembering the whispered conversation he'd heard between The General and Gemma this afternoon.

The young reporter scooted away and busied herself with cleaning more glasses. Theroux rounded the bar, his hungry gaze all over Gemma.

Goddamn, now this was what Waller called entertainment.

But there was something else to Theroux's glance. Was he angry?

A few minutes later, when it was clear that Gemma wasn't about to acknowledge her boss, Theroux shrugged, waved to Roxy and disappeared upstairs.

That's when the object of Waller's affection saw him.

"Well, look who's back," Roxy said, setting before him the drink Gemma had gotten from the skinny bartender and passed off to her.

Even though he would love to sit here and make small talk, Waller knew it was time to get started on the story. When he'd returned home last night, he'd scribbled some minor notes and possible questions before going to sleep.

Tonight, he intended to get to the meat of the matter.

"Couldn't resist this place," he said. "It's got a special air about it."

"We try to keep it smelling better than the likes of the tourist drag." Roxy smiled, her light brown eyes sparkling. "This here used to be the house of a rich man's mistress, back in the old days. Wealthy fellows used to go to the quadroon balls to choose young girls for their liking. Then the man would sign a contract with the girl's mama, keeping her and the daughter in good shape for years to come. As a matter of fact, the both of them would be provided for during the rest of their lives.

"Folks say that when Julia Dejan lived here, the house used to have some color to it, flowers in a court-yard out back and a light always glowing in the windows. By the time my boss took it over, it'd grown so old it couldn't even begin to look pretty anymore."

There. The mention of Theroux. An open door.

"Why doesn't the boss make an effort?" he asked.

"Damien's a busy boy. Got a lot going on that has nothing to do with giving dying houses a face-lift."

Now Waller just had to finesse this, make his questions seem perfectly natural. "What's more important than beautifying the *Vieux Carré?*"

The Old Square—the French Quarter.

Roxy was giving him the once-over. After Waller stopped reveling in it, he wondered if she'd been told to stay tight lipped about Theroux. It would only make sense.

"Funny how people like to talk around their own lives," Roxy said. "I find, being in the bar business, that men who do that often have the most to reveal."

Had he been tagged? This was a record for speed.

He spread his arms, making sure he emphasized his clean shirt. "I'm at your disposal, Roxy. What do you want to know?"

The subtle lift of her brow told him she'd noticed the care he'd taken with his wardrobe today. When she answered, he thought it was because she was rewarding him.

"I suppose it's slow enough in here for me to yap."

"I promise," he said, turning on the charm, rusty as it was, "I'll let you go as soon as you need to leave. I'm just in the market for some quality conversation."

"Well, then, Waller Smith, I'd like to know why you like to give my Gem a hard time around the bar."

Damn, he hadn't thought that their tension was so evident. "I barely know the girl." Which was true.

"You seem to upset her. She's a nice one, that Gem. Hard worker, and I like that about a person."

"I respect that, too," he half muttered.

Did he really treat Duncan that badly? Sure, he'd been riding her lately. Maybe that was a terrible thing to do. Maybe he should leave her alone to get all the recognition, all the accolades, this story would bring.

Waller paused, his mind reeling.

God, he wanted all that, too. So damned badly he could taste it. Wanted to feel good about himself again when he woke up in the mornings. Wanted to be proud of his headlines, his work ethic.

"I can be nicer to Gem," he said. "I didn't realize I was being such a jerk."

"Aw, Waller," Roxy said, beaming as she patted his hand, "I was hoping you'd say that."

His skin tingled where she'd touched it and, immediately, wanting to preserve the innocent sensation, Waller clasped his palm over it—trapping the feeling just in case it went away.

He stayed like that as the bar grew busier and Roxy went about her business. And the thing of it was, he felt like she'd infused him with a dose of optimism.

Waller Smith actually started to believe that maybe—just maybe—he could start to like himself again.

And pinning a big story on his lapel would no doubt make him feel even better.

6

AFTER HOURS, GEMMA WALKED out of a neighborhood bar down the street from Cuffs where she'd been killing time. She took shelter around the corner, checking to see if her place of employment was closed up and deserted by now.

Affirmative.

As she extracted tennis shoes and latex gloves from her big bag, she peeked around some more.

No one was near. Perfect! Time to get down to some real research.

In Theroux's empty office.

While donning her shoes and gloves, she couldn't help swallowing a lump of guilt lodged in her throat. Couldn't help chiding herself about how she'd handled him earlier. She hadn't set out to ignore him so thoroughly; it'd merely been a condition of innate shyness that had enveloped her, keeping her from acknowledging what had happened in the hallway.

But, still, there'd been a bright side to the night. During her usual bout of chatting up the customers, she'd uncovered a nugget of information.

A freckled African-American regular, wearing a

porkpie hat with a feather, had mentioned a gaming room. But he hadn't revealed its location. No matter how hard she'd tried to wheedle questions into the conversation, he hadn't come around and given it to her.

"You're too sweet and young to be gambling away your money, baby," he'd said, winking at her.

So that was why, an hour after closing, she was breaking into Theroux's office.

Knowing she was about to cross a jagged line, she uneasily approached Cuffs, which was dark and moody with silence. Locked.

No problem there. Having a big brother to show you things that would eventually get you into trouble definitely helped. In fact, when Gemma had gotten her first reporting job in Orange County, Jimmy had purchased a pick set for her as one of his practical jokes.

Well, hardy-har-har. She'd mastered the art of breaking and entering, keeping the tools in her huge shoulder bag and using them to unlock her own doors whenever she left her keys inside the house. She'd even surprised Jimmy once by letting herself into his home while he'd been chasing his wife around the kitchen in his Spider-Man boxers. But, up until tonight, she'd never sneaked into a place that was off-limits.

Blowing out an anxious breath, she inched her way over a small fence leading to the building's rear courtyard. From there, she stole up the gallery steps and picked the easy lock.

She'd checked for an alarm system earlier. Surprisingly, Cuffs didn't have one. Then again, who'd be stupid enough to rob a man like Damien Theroux?

Yeah, she thought, opening the door and flicking on a tiny flashlight, who'd be stupid enough to break into his place?

Though the hinges groaned, she managed to sneak in, creep down the hallway. His office was unlocked, too.

Trusting soul, wasn't he?

As she tiptoed toward his desk, her adrenaline raced, pushed by the thought of what she might discover. The scent of him filled the room—filled *her.* Even when he wasn't around, he scrambled her common sense, her overloaded libido.

With a determined huff of breath, she pushed her useless personal life aside and opened the first drawer. And that's when she heard it.

Breathing from a corner of the room.

A gasp ripped through her as she brought the flashlight around.

A cowering Waller Smith waved back at her. "Hello."

"Smith! What're you doing here?"

"Same thing you are, but I hid in the mop room while Roxy closed up. I didn't have to bulldoze my way in, unlike some naive reporters." His ruddy face flushed under the unforgiving beam of her light. "Mind putting that thing away?"

She kept it trained on him, just to be ornery. Smith held up a hand, shielding his eyes.

"I'm an employee of Cuffs," she said. "My presence in my boss's office is a little less suspect than yours."

"Come off it. It's not like you're going to find much, anyway. I snuck up here just as those kids finished having sex in the next room, then broke into the computer."

Gemma had seen the same two people from last night come upstairs earlier, but they weren't "kids" by any means. Had Smith seen additional customers? Forget it, for now. She wanted to know what was in the computer. When Smith was awake, he was actually pretty good at being the office tech nerd, but you had to catch him between z's.

"Did you hack in, or something?" In Gemma's growing excitement, she moved the light beam away from him.

"Thanks for saving my peepers." He came out of his corner. "I did my thing with this outdated hunk of junk. And, I'll tell you, Theroux must use an accountant, because he doesn't keep any questionable records here. He does a lot of stock-market speculation and legitimate real-estate transactions, though."

"Is that you sharing information with me, Smith?"

The older man chuffed. "If I had any, you wouldn't hear it. I'm just telling you not to waste your time, Duncan. You're going to have to dig deeper than this office if you want to crack Theroux."

Not trusting this nice version of her competitor, Gemma reached into a drawer, leafed through a ledger. She took out a digital camera and zoomed in for some pictures. Of what, she wasn't sure. She'd check the details later.

In the meantime, Smith shrugged and made for the door. "You're not going to see anything I haven't seen. Best of luck. That's about all you have on your side right now."

She refrained from tossing a comment—or a fond

gesture—his way as he left. Was the dolt taking the stairway? Good god, he'd better not tip anybody off to her presence by being careless.

Dammit, now she was under more stress than ever. Smith had gotten here first. He really was going to scoop her, wasn't he? And where would she be then?

While she shuffled through papers—indeed finding nothing terribly interesting—she did come across a hand-printed note, one that had been placed on Theroux's desktop, bold as you please. It seemed like a mock-up for an advertisement of some sort.

Dante's Basement
Invitation Only
Check Your Innocence at the Door

Sounded like a bad enterprise to her, so she took another picture and decided it was time to leave.

What a bust—except for this one intriguing piece of the puzzle.

Before leaving, she called a cab for a ride to her apartment in the Garden District. Then, on her way out, she vowed to discover what Dante's Basement was— and what Theroux had to do with it.

But how was she going to get the story before Smith found it first?

A very wicked idea formed in her head.

Theroux's sizzling touch. The way he'd held her, as if in complete enthrallment, after she'd pleasured herself in front of him.

There were other ways of gaining information,

weren't there? But could Gemma use everything she had at her disposal to get it?

Even while her good-girl upbringing screamed for her not to use sex as a lock pick, everything else in her body told her it was the only way to succeed over Smith.

And a way to satisfy all her pent-up curiosity about Theroux.

ACROSS THE STREET, DAMIEN leaned against the windowsill that decorated one of his properties. He had houses, land lots and businesses all over the city. Investments. Most of the places stood empty, waiting for a purpose, sadly greeting him whenever he visited to take stock of them.

He'd bought this brick structure on Burgundy Street because of its proximity to Cuffs. It was good for relaxation and reflection, though too much of both would drive Damien mad.

Much as Gem was doing.

He watched as her figure appeared on the sidewalk a half hour after she'd first gone inside. Damien had thought he'd seen another intruder—the new customer who always had cherry-Life Savers-like rings around his tired eyes—near the area just after she'd entered. Careful as always, Damien had phoned Kumbar, who'd just settled into his own bed, to check into the new customer.

But right now, his focus was only on Gem.

The woman who would help him even as she betrayed him.

He still couldn't believe it. Wasn't he a better judge

of character? How had Gem blinded him to her intentions so thoroughly? Something about her had gotten to him, and he wanted to shred through that weakness, destroy it before it destroyed him.

His life held no room for even one more tender, unchecked moment like the one he'd felt with her last night.

As she lingered under the awning, Damien quietly abandoned his house, walking up behind her, wondering if she'd found the little message left on his desk just in case she paid a reporter's visit to his purposely unlocked office.

He'd known she'd be doing it soon enough. After all, she'd probably been snooping in his private room last night, hadn't she? That's why she'd been in the hallway—because she'd wanted to uncover some dirt, some gossip for her newspaper.

Well, she would get it.

As he approached her, his shadow covered her body, and he decided to play this as if he wasn't as pissed as hell at her, as if he didn't know what she was up to.

"It's dangerous, meeting again like this," he said.

She jumped about twenty inches away from him. "Theroux?" Shaking her head, she recovered. "You've got a really bad habit of scaring the hell out of me. Can't you approach me like a normal person? Maybe clear your throat, or something, just so I don't get a coronary every time?"

"You're here late tonight."

"And you're here all the time." She hesitated, clearly not wanting to address his comment. Then she gave in.

"I had a tipple at Laffite's Blacksmith Shop. Can't help being drawn to tourist traps like that bar."

"Nobody's ever told you that a lone, beautiful woman walking around the streets at night is easy pickings?" He gestured at her feet. "Even if she is wearing running shoes?"

Obviously relieved that he wasn't pursuing the reason she was still here, Gem smiled, melting him a little.

Even though he knew better.

But some people just had smiles that did that to you, he supposed—made you feel like the center of the universe. He hadn't met many people with a smile so powerful. Knowing that Gem had an ulterior motive to be using it on him put Damien on even greater guard.

"Those pumps kill my feet," she said. "After work, I can't stand to be in my three-inch torture machines another minute, so I bring tennies to wear after my shift. It's a waitressing thing."

Down the street, headlights flashed over the cottages and brick houses, robbing his attention.

"You taking a cab, Gem?"

"Yeah. Saving up for a car of my own. I take the streetcars…um, everywhere else."

Probably to her newspaper office. "Why don't I take you on home?"

She seemed stunned by his offer, and he couldn't blame her. No doubt she wanted to keep him—the big story—away from her personal life. But Damien had more than a simple ride in mind.

This was step one of owning Gemma Duncan, twisting her to whatever he needed the reporter to be for him.

It was business as usual, with the same methods that always worked.

Manipulation. Painting people into a corner.

Complete domination.

He ran a thorough glance over his willing victim—the long blond hair withering out of its clip to her shoulders, the bar-darling tank and skirt.

Already he was getting hot for her again. The smoothness of her skin, the smell of it, never left him. He wasn't going to rest until he finally got this woman underneath him.

He could see that her eyelids had lowered slightly, weighed down with an answering desire, as if she was remembering how he'd brought out the wicked games in her yesterday.

"You want to take me home? Theroux, I—"

The cab's arrival cut her off, and without waiting for her to give permission, he paid the man a nice kiss-off fee, then led a speechless Gem to his car parked near the Burgundy Street house.

When she saw that it was a Ford Galaxie 500, a dark blue rebel cruiser with a fifties attitude and fins on the back, Gem laughed.

As she climbed in, she said, "I expected a Rolls-Royce with tinted windows. Not this."

"Stop expecting, then." He fired up the vehicle. "Where to?"

She paused. "You can drop me off on Fourth and Coliseum."

She wasn't going to show him where she lived. Cautious girl.

Pointing out the obvious, he said, "The Garden District." He cruised the streets, the purr of the motor petting the night. "The American sector."

"I found a steal for an apartment." Her voice became animated. "It's in the historic district. Wood floors. Live oaks right outside. I feel like I'm living in a fantasy world, even though the pipes are rusty and the walls are thin."

"You're still in your tourist phase of living here." He couldn't help but be attracted to her spirit, her love of his city. He shouldn't have been, but he would get over it soon enough.

"I don't think I'll ever change," she said. "There's something new to discover here day by day. Don't you feel that way about New Orleans? I mean, in most cities, the run-down buildings would be slums. Here, it's history. It's so—" she moved her shoulders in a sexy wave, searching for the word "—evocative."

This romantic streak would've seeped into his chinks if he'd been in the mood. Or maybe not. Damien had never allowed trivialities to affect him.

In an attempt to drive the sentimentality away, he mocked it. "Is that what makes you feel good?" he asked. "Shabby, dirty things?"

Her heard her swallow. Saw her tuck a strand of hair back with a nervous hand.

"If you're talking about last night," she said, staring out the windshield, "yeah. I was into it. I think you were, too."

"Oh, indeed I was. Watching a cat in heat does something to a fellow."

If he'd expected her to be offended, she surprised him.

As she turned to him, she had a confident, lopsided grin on her face, a seductive gleam to her gaze. "I have the feeling you're looking for something shabby and dirty to get you off, also, Damien."

She'd near whispered his name, handling it with practiced ease, as if she knew just what to do with such a personal part of him.

Thing was, she was right. He'd been looking for something new to please him for a while now. His customers' wives didn't do the trick. Neither did all the one-night stands who crossed his path.

Then again, this reporter probably just wanted to bang some information out of him. Not that he should complain.

"What would work for you, Gem?" he asked, baiting her. "What would turn you on so much that I'd be a happy man just watching you enjoy it?"

"A fantasy?"

"That would do."

"Let me think about it." And she turned back to her side of the car, folding her hands in her lap, seemingly teasing him with a cool attitude.

He smiled, and not pleasantly, either.

Neither of them spoke while he left the Quarter and crossed Canal, heading uptown.

As they drove up St. Charles Avenue, with its antebellum mansions and landscaped yards, Gem finally spoke.

"Don't drop me off just yet. Keep going."

And he did, taking a detour into areas where students from Loyola and Tulane universities lived.

"What makes me happy," she said, leaning an arm on the back of her seat and watching him, "is being in the middle of a crowded room while a man works me up. It has to do with being discovered, I think."

No doubt.

Though she seemed breezy about the scenario, Damien could see the anticipation behind her gaze. Could see that she was testing him—and maybe even herself.

"Not your thing?" she asked. "I've got a million more where that came from."

As they glided past a slim house with coral shutters and pink paint, Damien pulled over. Bright light and Led Zeppelin spilled out of the open windows. Untrimmed bushes lined the walkway. College-age partyers sprawled on the raised porch, plastic Budweiser cups in hand.

Without a word, he sent Gem a challenging glance, then started to get out of the car.

"You've got to be kidding," she said. "We're going to a kid party?"

As a response, he opened her door and helped her out, her skin searing his as he clasped her hand.

Boy. When they finally made it to a mattress, there were going to be some fireworks. Some payback.

He guided her past the iron fence and up the path to the house. Even though they received a few curious glances on the way inside—Damien didn't exactly scream "collegiate" with his dark, expensive suit and jaded gaze—they made it to the center of the room without a fuss. Maybe it was because there were three professorial-looking men talking with coeds near the kitchen, making the age issue moot.

A drunk kid ogled Gem's skimpy black top as he pushed beers at them. They both refused, and when the fellow tried to engage her in conversation, all Damien had to do was look hard at him to scare the bozo off.

"What now?" Gem asked. "Are these friends of yours?"

"Nah." Some girls in tube tops and braids were bouncing on a couch in time to "Immigrant Song." Though what was falling out of their stretchies would've pleased many a man, Damien kept his eyes on Gem.

"Then why're we here?" she asked.

With a cursory look, Damien inspected the room— the threadbare Salvation Army chairs, the stained carpet, the party-is-almost-done urgency on some of the faces. In a distant corner by a half-empty bookshelf, he found the unmanned bar. Plastic cups dotted the surface like smokestacks from a river steamer.

"We're here," he said, talking over the music, "because I'm up to any game you want to play."

And he meant that in more than one way.

Then, with negligent command, he ran his knuckles over the crest of one breast. Gem drew in a quick breath, then sent him a gaze that confirmed she was upping the ante.

Lips parted, beach-baby-blue eyes all but hidden under long, mascara-teased lashes, she said, "Then let's go."

"Dancing Days," with its winding, snake-charmer

guitar licks, accompanied them as Damien led her behind that bar, positioning her so she faced the crowd. He stood behind her with his hands on her shoulders, kneading her skin until she lazily moved with every stroke.

Gemma knew he was just warming up for…something. What had she been thinking when she'd confessed one of her most forbidden fantasies to him? She hadn't ever been a public-display-of-affection type of girl—ever.

So why had the thought of getting away with intimacy in front of other people flipped her skirt? *Was* it because of the secrecy? The risk of getting caught?

Was it just like breaking into someone's office or pretending to be what you weren't?

She sighed, wishing she could just block out the job and concentrate on him—the man she was out to get.

As Damien pressed his body to her back, she could feel him getting hard. Well, she was flaming up, too, just from the thought of strolling into this party and…

He slipped his hands down her arms, sensitizing them until her fine hairs stood on end. "See that kid across the room?" he asked.

Gemma nodded because that was the only way she could communicate right now.

It was the blond student who'd tried to give them beer. Not much older than twenty-one, he was using the wall to hold him and his Slim Shady T-shirt up. He was giving her that awful-drunkard, do-you-think-I'm-sexy? stare.

Did every university have a How to Get Laid 101 course where this misguided look was part of the syllabus?

"He likes you," Theroux said. "He's been watching you ever since you came in. Poor boy can't help it."

Without warning, Theroux swept one hand down the back of her thigh and laughed, probably more from how her legs were buckling than how she had a secret admirer in the room. When he traced his fingertips back and forth, she got even weaker, skin tingling, belly clutching.

Gemma wondered how far she'd let him go. And when he trailed his fingers between her inner thighs, she wondered again.

Then he coasted upward, sketching along her lace-covered cleft. Bucking, she collapsed onto the bar, breathless, resting her chin in her palm, trying to act as if nothing was going on. Avoiding eye contact with Shady Boy.

Remember, she told herself, getting closer to Theroux gets you closer to what you need. Lovers know more about each other than anyone.

Now he was sliding his fingers backward, under the elastic in the bottom of her underwear, thumb memorizing the curve of her rear. A finger whisked back under the lace, against her wetness this time, and Gemma closed her eyes, wanting to sob just once. Yeah, one sob would help.

"You get ready for me to enter you so fast, Gem," he said, timing a few more strokes—harder, then harder still—to the sinuous beat of the music.

Then, before she could suck in another breath, he

grabbed her undies with that one hand and jerked them down.

Oh. Oooohhhh.

Trying to be casual—because, frankly, Shady Boy was starting to watch them with a different kind of stare now—Gemma kept leaning on her palm. At the same time, she let out a fake, tension-releasing laugh, then reached back and cupped Theroux's midnight-stubble cheek with her other hand, just as though they were getting cozy here in the corner, and that was all.

Sweet coziness. Nothing going on here.

Other than Shady Boy, no one else in the room seemed to be aware of them as Theroux got to his knees, totally hidden by the bar. After he lowered her underwear all the way, she stepped out of it. He spread her legs, moving to the front of her and smoothing his hands up her thighs.

What if someone decided they wanted a drink? What if someone came around the corner and saw…?

She was pounding, pained with sharp yearning.

As he pushed her skirt up, air tickled the pulsing center of her, making her so vulnerable. Near her knees, his slow kisses added to the nerve-tingling sensations, branding her inner thighs with heat and quaking need.

She leaned both elbows on the bar, not trusting herself to stand anymore. A trickle of her juices meandered downward, and he licked it, bathing her skin with his tongue.

Covering her face with her hand, she forced herself to act as if she was just standing here, having a great old college-party time. In reality, she knew she was blushing uncontrollably, overheating and probably grinning like a dazed doll.

He was pressing his erection against her shin and, unthinkingly, she rubbed against the stiffness, up, down, encouraging him, needing him to go higher, to…

Yes, higher. While gnawing at the crease between her thigh and her sex, he took a thumb to her clit, circling it and guiding one of her legs over his shoulder to open her even more. She didn't have to look down to know that her skirt was all the way up in front. The image of him buried against her caused a flash of damp heat to explode.

As she rocked against his mouth, she felt the vibration of his laugh. This time, the buzz of erotic motion almost *did* make her cry.

Instead, she bit her palm, since it was still against her face.

All her blood was rushing down, lightening her head to dizziness, convincing her that if she cried out at the top of her lungs, it wouldn't matter.

She was just about to when Shady Boy popped up in front of her. He was barely visible between her fingers.

Go away.

"Hellooooo," he said.

Unable to form coherent speech patterns, she sighed on a groan.

"Where'd your friend go?" he asked.

Beneath the bar, Theroux delved into her, sucking, swirling his tongue, drinking her in. She couldn't help moving her hips with his every kiss.

"He's…coming…" she managed, thinking that, no, she had that all wrong.

She was doing all the coming.

And…here it went. Her sight dimmed and flashed back on, a warped movie in a malfunctioning projector. Losing it… Losing…

Pressure built, pooling, boiling. The slide of his tongue against her only made things worse.

No, better.

She closed her eyes, blacking out the theater of her sight, making her mind a whirring vacuum of sensation.

Gemma slumped over the bar, hand over her face again.

Shady Boy thunked to the wood, too.

Suddenly a spark burst in her machinery, an explosion of flame and destruction, devouring her from the inside out. Bursting into a bonfire of melted form, reduced to liquid.

Waves upon waves of sin and release. An unspooled strip of film, flapping as the projector kept going round and round.

Thank goodness Shady Boy had clammed up, passed out with his head next to hers. As for Theroux—

Gemma felt her skirt being fixed back into place, and she rolled her head to the side, too spent to move anymore.

He'd changed position, his hand on one of her ankles. Now, he was crouched by her leg, a look of raw hunger making his pale eyes more feral than ever.

He was holding her underwear, rubbing it between his thumb and forefinger as if the lace were her skin. A shudder consumed her, and he smiled, pocketing the reminder of her fantasy.

One that had obviously worked for both of them.

7

THE NEXT DAY IN DAMIEN'S office, he couldn't get a lick of work done.

Lick. There he went again.

He could still taste her, even the morning after. Could still feel the glide of his mouth while he brought her home.

And what had that made him? Something like a walking dildo that existed for only one thing—the need to slide into a woman.

He hated the turnabout. It was just one more betrayal, one more crumbling weakness. At this rate, Gem would have *him* under her thumb. As it was, after their close encounter behind the bar, he'd been ready for more. So much more. But she'd merely smiled, tucked her hair into place and asked to leave the party.

Oh, he'd been roused for some action then, yes, sir, but Gem obviously hadn't been thinking along the same lines.

"You were wonderful, Damien," she'd said, holding on to his car door as he'd dropped her off on the designated corner. "If you're a good boy, maybe there'll be another fantasy after work tomorrow."

And he'd had to settle for that.

Damien stared into space for a while longer, thinking about Gem's black underwear. When he'd gotten back to his home on Esplanade Avenue, he'd laid the delicate material in a drawer by his bedside. Unfortunately, he'd been thinking about those lacies to such a degree that he hadn't gotten a wink of sleep.

His cell phone rang, bringing him back to the moment.

It was Kumbar, and once again, Damien didn't like the news his man had uncovered about Waller Smith.

"Another reporter." He closed up his phone and tossed it to the surface of his desk, right on top of the faux Dante's Basement announcement. Apparently, Smith, reporter #2 to infiltrate his life, had seen it when *he'd* broken into Damien's office.

Just as Gem had.

Dante's Basement. A place that didn't exist. Not yet, at least. If Gem took this bait, though, a decadent club of forbidden fantasies would come to life, if only to shape her perception of how wicked Damien Theroux could be.

Put that in your paper, chérie, he thought, narrowing his eyes.

Half of him hoped she would pursue this false bit of information. Half of him hoped he could trust her not to.

The weak half of him, Damien decided.

Dammit, where had all these journalists come from, anyway? And why was he all of a sudden so interesting to them?

The fact that they weren't wary enough to keep their distance, as they had in the past, concerned Damien.

But, even worse, he wondered if Gem and Smith were a team, working together to expose him.

He pressed a button on an intercom connected to the bar downstairs. "Roxy?"

A few seconds passed before a familiar drawl greeted him. "Right here, Dam."

"Come on up, would you?"

"I'm on my way."

He sat back in his chair, devising all sorts of ways to handle this Waller Smith. Jean Dulac, having been raised to be a big boss someday, would advise Damien to rough up the reporter. Kumbar might even think the same thing. But Damien didn't have much of a taste for violence.

Not unless it was the only way out.

"You're looking fit to strangle someone," Roxy said, entering the office and propping a hand on a well-padded hip. The ceiling fan played with her red hair, running the strands over pale skin too youthful to belong to a forty-six-year-old.

"What do you know about our new barfly? Waller Smith?"

Roxy perked up. Damien's eyebrows rose at her reaction.

"Old Waller," she said, smiling and tilting her head. "Why, he's shifty in a way, but cute as can be. Very charming, with kind eyes and lots of wrinkles that tell some stories I'd like to hear. Why you asking about the man?"

In the six years he'd owned Cuffs, Roxy had taken

to her share of customers, but Damien didn't recall her ever being so sparkling about one.

Sparkling. What a word. But it was the only way to describe the way she was…beaming.

Did he ever look like that? Was there a noticeable difference in him ever since he'd met Gem?

Damien sat forward in his chair, moving away from such a dumb question. There was no reason for him to be sparkling about a woman—especially the undercover reporter.

Sex, and whatever went with it, was just a way to improve or sustain your life. It wasn't some magic cure for the blues, wasn't anything more than two people getting together to feel better about themselves.

"I've got some reservations about your friend," he said, a rough edge to his voice. Frustration. Anger. Whatever he was carrying around inside these days besides the normal program for revenge. "Does he ask a lot of questions?"

"More than the usual." Roxy's forehead wrinkled, waiting for some bad news.

Damien hadn't told her about Gem being a reporter yet, hadn't told her about his plans to manipulate her story. It was time, he supposed.

After he revealed Gem's betrayal, Roxy's shoulders slumped. "Are you certain?"

"Kumbar's got the best resources. I'm certain."

She looked crushed, and Damien hated to add to her sadness.

"Come to find out, Waller Smith is one of them, too. A reporter."

"Him? Old Waller? So he was plucking me like a fiddle with all them compliments and…"

She trailed off, and something human within Damien felt compelled to pat her shoulder, to say words that would make her feel better.

Two years ago, Roxy had gone through a terrible divorce. The proceedings had decimated her self-esteem, though you would never know it from her apparent confidence with the customers. Roxy loved her work, though, separating it from her personal life. While in the bar, she believed she was a different woman—"the hostess with the mostess," she'd say—than the "dowd" at home, or in the grocery store shopping for her two teenage sons.

"Is Waller more than a customer to you?" Damien asked, trying to offer some kind of comfort. Damn, he was bad at this. But at least he was trying to lead up to making her feel better.

Awful at hiding her emotions, Roxy gazed at the carpet. "I was hoping… Aw, everyone in Cuffs is just a customer, you know that. Just because Waller was good at making me blush and giving me the interested eye don't mean much."

"A lot of fellows give you that eye, Rox."

She pushed away the compliment with a wave of the hand. "Go on, now. You're too busy staring at Gem to see what goes on anymore."

A thrust of remembrance filled him. Last night. Skin. Heat. Gem coming because he'd made her do it.

"Listen," he said, changing the subject to keep himself on track. He reached for his check ledger and pen.

"I need a favor from you. We're going to keep Gem and Waller around because I can use some bad publicity." In particular, Bundy Sonnier, a fellow game-room owner who didn't seem to respect Damien or his protector from the Dulac family, crossed his mind. "Sonnier's been getting pretty brave lately. Last week, he sent some of his boys to my gaming room. They didn't do any damage, but I don't like where that might be headed. If they hear some stories about my awful temper and what I do to men who cross me, maybe they'll back off. And then there was Lamont and his threatening to go to the press about my charity work.... I don't need that sort of reputation."

With that, he cut a check and presented it to his head waitress. "Maybe you can talk to Waller about my darker side, eh? And maybe a flirting touch or two from you wouldn't hurt."

Roxy's amber eyes looked like bourbon that had been served with too much ice. She ignored the check. "You hiring me out, Damien? Just like a whore?"

"I'm not in that business."

"Oh, I'm well aware, baby." She hesitated, standing on her tiptoes, peeking at the amount on the paper. "This is important to you, then."

"Very." He stuck the check out farther. "This'll help pay for some of the kids' college tuition."

He could tell she was fighting with herself, a battle between pride and need. Finally, she took the paper, staring at it as if it were the enemy.

"Just throw Waller Smith off my scent," he reiterated, "and I'll treat you well, Rox. In fact, invite him to Club

Lotus tonight. He'll accept. But don't you worry about Gem. I'll be taking care of her."

"I've no doubt of it."

Again, he hardened right up, remembering Gem's promise from last night.

If you're a good boy, maybe there'll be another fantasy after work tomorrow.

A fantasy he would construct this time.

Dante's Basement. Something just for Gem. Something to show her how nasty he could be, and to distract her from the reality of Club Lotus. He didn't want her there to witness the fleecing, the hatred that drove him.

And why was that?

He didn't stop to think. Wouldn't stop to think.

Roxy started to walk out of the office, but turned around, flashing the check at him for emphasis.

"You look pretty satisfied with yourself right now, but I'd hate to be around when you find that power ain't happiness, Damien."

He tried to arrange his body, his face, to show that he hadn't already suspected this was true. But that only happened in his weaker moments, when he also wondered why he needed to bleed those CEOs, to take great satisfaction out of their losses.

Roxy didn't allow his unaffected air to stop her from getting the entire sermon out. "I know you loved your father. But he took his own life, baby. He died by his own devices. You can't keep wanting revenge for what he did to himself."

Damien could barely get the words past his tight jaw. "Those men—just like the ones I invite to my club—killed him sure enough. Driving someone to their death because they're too damned ashamed to live is the same as murder in my book."

Roxy sent him a sympathetic glance, and Damien refused to acknowledge it. When his *papa*'s ex-employers had drained his retirement account through their greed and scams, it'd taken the life right out of Martin Theroux.

His son just wanted to make sure it didn't happen on his home turf. Not to any other families.

Never again.

"What will you be," she asked softly, "when you lose your power over people? That's all I want to know."

When he didn't respond, Roxy left, shutting the door behind her. Damien didn't try to think of answers, because there were none. How could there be in a world where he could never bring his father back?

That's all *he* wanted to know.

JUST BECAUSE IT WAS A WEEKEND, didn't mean Gemma had the day off.

At Cuffs, she would have Mondays and Tuesdays all to herself, but every day was reporter day. Good thing she hadn't given Jerome Lamont a rest, either, because when he'd exited his Dumaine Street courtyard this morning, she'd been waiting patiently for him, notepad and recorder at the ready.

He'd been about as happy to see her as a dog facing a determined army of fleas, but she didn't mind. Reporters had to live with resistance.

And remorse.

As she'd walked to The Court of Two Sisters with him—he was meeting a friend for jazz brunch—she'd nevertheless done the whole eyelash-batting, this-is-the-right-thing-to-do wheedling act. Finally, he'd broken down a little, inadvertently revealing the name of Theroux's gaming room.

Club Lotus.

Hah! Now, she just had to locate the address and get into the place, track down some people who knew the inner secrets of it. And maybe, just maybe, with a little more cajoling and pursuing, Lamont would really start opening up to her. Sure, he'd started to sweat copiously before scuttling away from her into the restaurant, but she could get him to talk.

If he could get over the whole Theroux-ain't-a-man-to-cross belief.

For the rest of the day, she'd scoured the Quarter, even paying some college kids to enter bars "undercover" and find out how to gain entrance into Club Lotus, but to no avail. By that time, her second job beckoned.

Cuffs.

Roxy caught Gemma just as she was stowing her belongings in the supply room and tying on her short apron.

"Boss wants to see you," the redhead said, occupying herself by folding a load of clean bar towels. "Might as well get it done before the crowds show up."

"Will do." Gemma grinned at Roxy, but the woman was as busy as an ant before winter, taking only enough time to nod at her before dashing out of the room.

Was Roxy in a bad mood? Or…?

If Roxy knew she was a reporter, then Theroux knew, and…

Oh. Was that why he wanted to see her?

She took a moment to gather her courage. Then she reached into her apron pocket and removed her mini-tape recorder, securing it behind some dusty liquor that hadn't been approached in years, grabbed her pepper spray and shoved it into the recorder's place.

Finally, she climbed those stairs, stomach a nest of buzzing energy. The nervous warmth traveled downward, coating her with memories of the party—of what had happened behind the bar.

Okay, yes, she was embarrassed about the intimacy, but she was desperate for more, too. But besides all that, sex was a weapon for her. A way to get to him.

Dammit, why did that sound so terrible?

And the Pulitzer goes to…

There. Strong again. Chin up, she lightly knocked on Theroux's office door.

"Come on in," drawled that bayou-water voice.

All right, ace. Don't drop the ball. Ask him about Dante's Basement. You forgot all about it last night.

She wouldn't allow her body to overcome her mind again. Nope. Not today. She was on *fire*.

When she entered, he had one leg propped over the other, the ledger balanced on the top one. Dressed in his favorite color, he reminded Gemma of a gothic hero sitting in front of a halfway shuttered window. A peek of dusk settled through the opening, burnishing the oil paintings, the walls.

She put on a confident act, as if she was the one who held all the cards. "How's it going?"

It took a few moments for him to glance up at her. Every tick of her watch marked a thudding heartbeat.

Would it be a bad thing to dive over his desk to get to him? To straddle his lap and relieve the tight lust that had been gathering in her body all day?

Finally, just as she was really contemplating it, he closed the ledger and tossed it on his desktop. Then he leaned back in his chair, his eyes half-hooded in sleepy-sexy consideration. He motioned for her to sit, but she waved it off.

He didn't seem to mind. "Good to see you again, Gem."

All right. This could go any way. It could be an I-know-what-you-really-are moment or he could really be happy to see her.

"Likewise." She flashed a smile at him, all sweetlike. "Roxy sent me up. Is anything wrong?"

He leaned his head back and tapped the pen against his chin, never taking his eyes off her. "I'd say everything is going fine. Just fine."

So, the intensity was getting to her a little. She stepped closer, conquering her insecurity, wanting to wrap him around her pinkie finger. Moving in for the kill, she leaned down, bracing her hands on the desk, exposing some cleavage. For extra effect, she playfully swayed back and forth.

"Then what can I do for you?" she asked.

He liked what he heard. And saw. She could tell from his appreciative grin.

Even though she wasn't focusing on his desk, she could see the Dante's Basement flyer lying on the surface.

Don't forget why you're here.

"Last night," he said, allowing the words to hover like an afterglow mist sprinkling over her skin, "I didn't mention that I've got something to see to this evening."

Club Lotus? She knew it wasn't open every night, and he'd been around the last few. It was time for another round of gaming, then.

He added, "That means I won't be around."

Disappointment dive-bombed her body.

Man. Did she really need his attentions that much? Was she that addicted to him?

Yes. No. No, no, no.

She shrugged a bit, just to convince herself that it was no big thing. What a lie.

"So I guess I'll have to find another way to occupy myself," she said.

From the way his pale eyes darkened, she knew he was recalling her self-pleasure in the hallway.

"Maybe," she continued, pressing her arms together to create even more cleavage as she angled forward, "I'll even explore more of New Orleans." She nodded toward the Dante's Basement flyer. "Check your innocence at the door? Sounds interesting."

He nonchalantly turned over the paper. "That's not for you, Gem."

"Why not? Is it one of your clubs?"

Pausing, he tapped a finger on his desk. She couldn't help looking at his hands, fantasizing about how they'd strummed her last night.

"Do you know how I make my money?" he asked.

Yesssss. Here it went. She tried not to fall all over herself in excitement.

"There's Cuffs. I hear you own a restaurant and a souvenir shop or two."

"That's the tip of it."

His gaze caressed her breasts, and Gemma performed for all she was worth, encouraging him by drawing one hand over her chest as if she was wiping away a rivulet of sweat. It helped that his hot looks were stimulating her, bringing her nipples to hard peaks that she wanted him to kiss and suck.

Mamma mia. Wiped out by the mere possibility, she propped herself on the edge of his desk, watching him from over her shoulder. Absently, she fingered the hem of her short skirt, drawing his attention there.

Her success should have felt better, though.

"Besides the tame stuff," she asked, determined to carry this through, "what else do you own, Damien?" *Besides me,* she thought. *At least, my body. For right now.*

She could've sworn that his eyes had gone hazy. Was he reliving last night, too? Conjuring up new scenarios?

With a soft smile, she ran her thumb under her hem, lifting her skirt so her upper thigh was visible.

She looked away as he visually stroked her, too.

"You'll think less of me if I tell you what I'm really about," he said.

Yeah, as if he probably cared what she thought. "Of course I won't."

Another grin, but this time she could catch the ruthless sting of it.

"Let's just say I'm into the more intriguing side of life, Gem. Let's just say vice pays the rent nicely."

Widening her eyes, Gemma pretended to be shocked, but in a good way. "What does that mean? Are you some kind of criminal?"

Theroux held up his hands. *You caught me.* "That's for the cops to say. Me, I think I provide services that are very much in demand."

A-ha. This was why she was here—for the heroic stuff. The comeuppance of a bad man.

"What? Drugs?"

He raised his eyebrows. Could have been yes or no. When he didn't answer, she tried again.

"Prostitutes?"

This time, he took his time setting the pen on the desk, right next to the Dante's Basement announcement.

"Gambling?"

"Gaming. Here we call it 'gaming.' Gambling is illegal here, *chérie.*" He leaned back in his chair and folded his hands behind his head. "Besides, drugs, whores, gaming, they all go together."

"You *are* into them?" God, if she could only have this recorded. "Then, this Dante's? Is it a gaming club? Can I go? It sounds so James Bond."

"I don't think so, Gem. You stick to Cuffs. A girl like you shouldn't be messing with places of that nature."

Shot down. She could feel her momentum sliding.

Images flashed over her mind's eye: Theroux kneeling in front of her and spreading her legs wide. Theroux watching as she climaxed, enthralled. She could've asked him to do just about anything at that moment last night.

So why not use that to her advantage, even if it tore her in two?

"A girl like me?" She slid off the desk, walked around it like she was tracking him, headed for the back of his chair. With each step, he kept her in his own sights, and she wondered just who was hunting whom.

"You mean," she added, positioning herself behind him and gliding her palms down his hard chest, then back up, "a girl who likes a little danger?"

Under the silk of his shirt, she felt his nipples tighten. Springboarding off this sign of success, she rubbed them until he shifted.

A little danger. Her comment had been uncomfortably true, hadn't it? Suddenly, Gemma did feel scared, mostly because she wasn't sure what to expect of herself anymore.

"Gem," he said, voice slightly choked, "do you know what you're asking for?"

No. And yes.

"I want to know all about you—your work, your play. I want to know what gets *you* hot, Damien." Oh, it felt so good to say his name. A lilt of the exotic, a taste of sweet cream and spice.

"You're ready to see what amounts to a dark underworld?" He laughed, probably because it sounded so dramatic.

But this was his life, she thought. Criminal, illegal and below the radar.

With her finger, she traced his lips, concentrating on

the full lower one. Soft, but she'd known that last night, when his mouth had been pressed to her.

When he nipped at her, she teasingly removed the finger from his reach, then coasted it down the buttons of his shirt. *Pop, pop, pop,* the discs went under her touch.

"I'm more than ready to see what you're into," she said.

She wanted him again. So badly. Too badly. It took all her strength not to rub her cheek against his hair, to steal some affection along with the passion.

But that would be a huge mistake. A rookie move. Effective reporters were objective, cold and unbiased. And that was how she needed to be.

"If it'll please you, then I'll give you a taste of it," he said, clearly in tune to her sensual agitation. He grasped her wrist and started to lead her hand down his chest, lower, lower…. "Tomorrow night you'll have another fantasy, Gem. Danger. Dante's. But one thing."

She stopped him from guiding her hand below his belt, even though her fingers were itching to brush over him, just so she could get a hint of what she was missing. Longing for. "What? What's the caveat?"

Instead of forcing her hand over him, as she half expected, he maneuvered his fingers so they clasped hers. A surprising gesture, tender in its interruption of a more seductive game.

He kissed the back of her hand, then whispered against her knuckles. "Don't speak of Dante's to anyone. You understand? Never."

As his lips lingered, another bolt of guilt shook her.

And there was something else, too. Something even more empty and confusing.

The realization that, with all of their intimate games, she'd never actually kissed him.

8

WHILE THEROUX AND GEMMA were upstairs, her competition settled onto his now-regular bar stool at Cuffs, waiting for Wedge the bartender to bring him his gin and tonic.

Waller made himself comfortable, thinking that the stool fit him perfectly. His rear had shaped itself to the vinyl, knowing it'd found a decent partner.

And he deserved the rest, having worked pretty hard today at the *Weekly*. Besides doing some extensive database research about all the big gaming players in New Orleans, he'd accomplished two actual interviews for a different tabloid story. Surprisingly, he'd done a damned thorough job, too.

"Hubby and Wife Exchange Gunfire in Shotgun Home!" the headline would read. When the cops had come, it'd turned out that the two had been using their kids' BB guns as weapons, leveling accusations about each other's suspected affairs at the same time. It wasn't one of his more torrid pieces, but Waller thought he'd done an outstanding job of getting to the bottom of the couple's marital problems, the roots of their erratic behavior.

A good day. It'd been a real long time since he'd been able to say that. He just wished he could share his contentment with Roxy, maybe over a glass of wine, a dinner overlooking the moonlit river.

At the thought of being with her, Waller's body did the wave for the first time in years. It was like the Super Bowl in his belly—a screaming flow of chaos cheering him on. A pulsing yen for touch, a mind-boggling hankering for heat.

He glanced at his watch again. Just where was Roxy? A few more people had wandered into Cuffs, signaling that the rush was beginning. Shouldn't she be leaning on the bar across from him, flashing a grin that kept her forever young?

Not five minutes later, she showed up, zooming through the bar as if her hair were on fire.

On her next pass, Waller tried to flag her down. And...

Ignored.

Nice. Couldn't she even stop for a bit of chatter? She'd lavished him with it every night, staying a few more minutes each time. They'd gotten as far as talking about her teen boys, and how one liked model airplanes while the other liked fast cars. Then there was her divorce and, even though Roxy never bashed her ex, Waller could sense that there was a lot of pain there.

God, where was Duncan when he needed her? Shouldn't his fellow reporter be here helping Roxy, allowing her some comfort and a few seconds off her feet? He would talk to the young girl about giving her boss more of a hand.

And he didn't have long to wait. Soon, his rival descended the rickety stairs and, right away, Waller knew something was bothering her. She had her hands tucked in her apron pockets, a distracted look wrinkling her forehead. She'd pinned her blond hair up yet again, each escaped strand a victim of the humidity—wilted and damp.

But when she encountered her first set of customers, the patented Duncan charm came on full force. Bling. Just like a neon sign flickering to life and opening for business.

After she came to the bar to place an order, Waller caught her arm, just as surprised at the gesture as Duncan was.

"Everything kosher?" he asked.

Even more shocking, there was concern in his question.

Duncan hesitated and, for a second, Waller thought she was going to confide in him. Some kind of big-brother twang vibrated in the area of Waller's out-of-tune heart.

"Duncan?" he prodded.

Then she let out a tight sigh, adopting a bright smile. "It's nothing I can't handle, Smith." The perkiness disappeared. "You'd better get back to your...drink."

Waller lowered his voice, barely making it louder than the jukebox's rendition of "Honky Tonk Women."

"If you need some help, you just call. Got it?"

She shot him a skeptical glance, then paused, searching his face.

What was she seeing? The same man who winked at himself in the mirror this morning after he'd donned a

GET FREE BOOKS and a FREE GIFT WHEN YOU PLAY THE...

Just scratch off the silver box with a coin. Then check below to see the gifts you get!

SLOT MACHINE GAME!

YES! I have scratched off the silver box. Please send me the 2 free Harlequin Blaze™ books and gift for which I qualify. I understand I am under no obligation to purchase any books, as explained on the back of this card.

350 HDL D7W4   **150 HDL D7XJ**

FIRST NAME

LAST NAME

ADDRESS

APT.#	CITY

STATE / PROV.	ZIP/POSTAL CODE

7	7	7	Worth **TWO FREE BOOKS** plus a **BONUS Mystery Gift!**
🍒	🍒	🍒	Worth **TWO FREE BOOKS!**
♣	♣	♣	Worth **ONE FREE BOOK!**
🔔	🔔	🍒	**TRY AGAIN!**

www.eHarlequin.com

(H-B-04/05)

DETACH AND MAIL CARD TODAY!

The Harlequin Reader Service® — Here's how it works:

Accepting your 2 free books and gift places you under no obligation to buy anything. You may keep the books and gift and return the shipping statement marked "cancel." If you do not cancel, about a month later we'll send you 4 additional books and bill you just $3.99 each in the U.S., or $4.47 each in Canada, plus 25¢ shipping & handling per book and applicable taxes if any.* That's the complete price and — compared to cover prices of $4.75 each in the U.S. and $5.75 each in Canada — it's quite a bargain! You may cancel at any time, but if you choose to continue, every month we'll send you 4 more books, which you may either purchase at the discount price or return to us and cancel your subscription.

*Terms and prices subject to change without notice. Sales tax applicable in N.Y. Canadian residents will be charged applicable provincial taxes and GST. Credit or debit balances in a customer's account(s) may be offset by any other outstanding balance owed by or to the customer.

freshly ironed button-down and a dollop of aftershave so past its prime that it smelled more like *Ancient* Spice?

Maybe he'd changed in some indefinable way lately, but she sure hadn't. Reverting back to spunky reporterness, Duncan gave him a professional nod.

"I'm fine, Smith. But if *you* need help…"

"You'll come running." He toasted her with the drink. "True to form, Duncan, true to form."

"I've got all my ducks in a row," she said, starting to move away when she spied more customers entering.

She didn't have to say it. Waller knew exactly how she was planning to get her information. S-E-X. He'd seen it happen before in other newspaper offices. Had seen the toll it'd taken on the reporters' consciences, on their ethical balance.

Waller turned away from Duncan, unable to watch another one fall.

He jerked at the sight in front of him. Roxy, with a million questions in her gaze.

When he met her stare, she doffed her miffed demeanor so quickly that Waller wondered whether or not he'd seen it at all.

She was back to herself—the smiling welcome, the flirty body language.

"How're you tonight, Waller?"

Her southern voice dragged over him, like a woman's hair sliding over a man's chest. Silky, touching every last inch of his flesh.

Without thinking, Waller smoothed his own hair back from his forehead, hoping it looked as good as it had when he'd endlessly combed the pale mop in the

Weekly's restroom mirror. "I'm much better now that you're standing in front of me, Roxy. How's your day been?"

"Up and down, I'd say." Something flashed in her eyes, and she turned her gaze to the bar, rubbing at it with a small towel.

"Then I guess it's up to me to make the night better for you."

When she looked back up, Roxy seemed a little sad. "You're not such a bad sort, are you?"

Odd question. At any rate, she should ask his ex-wife about it. Not that he even knew where Tawny was living now. Who she was sleeping with, nagging at, trying to comfort after a tough day at work by drawing him a bath and caressing his troubles away with a water-steeped sponge and lather-soft platitudes.

Waller chased away the memories, the ineptitude of having failed to keep hold of a sweet woman who just couldn't take his former swan dive into bitterness anymore. A woman who couldn't relate to the same darkness he'd seen day after day as a crime reporter.

Right now, he didn't want to wallow in the past. He only wanted to cheer Roxy up. Pretty funny, considering his primary purpose for being in the bar wasn't to win a conquest. It was to put the screws to her boss—and, in effect, to her.

Just keep that in mind—you're using her, chump. Nice basis for a relationship.

"There's a lot I'd do for you, Roxy." He wiped some ice sweat off his full glass.

If I could.

And if he had any guts, he'd color inside the outlines of the heart he was wearing so clearly on his sleeve. Or should he get to work, wringing information out of this woman he was so attracted to?

Her answering laugh sounded like water in a courtyard fountain. It recaptured Waller's attention in a pulse beat.

"If my boss would let me off for the night," she said, positioning a hip against the bar so she wasn't facing him straight on, "I'd certainly take you up on your promise. I'd make you dance with me at a zydeco bar. Or I'd make you run out and get me some fresh daisies so I could look at them and remember that there's still a sun shining somewhere in the world."

Waller was torn between liberating her—showing her a night on the town she would never forget—or taking a step through a door she'd left wide open. Damien Theroux. She'd brought up the subject first.

Dammit, if he could get this story and show everyone that he wasn't a burned-out has-been without a future, maybe Waller could deserve a woman like Roxy. As it was now, he didn't exactly have much to offer someone as good as she seemed.

Would she actually give him information? And how loyal was Roxy to Theroux? Would she end up hating Waller for exposing her boss?

Incredibly, Roxy led him right to what he was looking for.

"I tell you," she said, picking at the nubs on her towel, "if I were to give in to my whims and step out that door right now, the boss would blow his top. You've never seen a temper like the one on Damien Theroux."

She gulped, kept her eyes on the towel.

Waller was too busy getting into his knight-in-shining armor to sense another reason for why she wouldn't meet his gaze.

"Does he unleash that temper on you, Roxy? If he does, I don't care how brutal he is. I'll—"

"Don't you dare." She'd clasped his hand. "Damien is as mean as a cottonmouth, quick and angry. Never anger him, Waller. You don't want to know what he does to people who cross him."

Oh, but he did.

Under Roxy's hand, Waller's skin flamed and tingled. He turned his palm over, the better to hold her fingers in his. Ah, there. A touch. Her weight resting in the cup of his hand.

Life was good.

She seemed to like it, too. A blush covered her delicate features, and she lightly ran her thumb against the side of his pinkie finger. Unbidden, she continued providing him with her innocent information.

"They say Damien once rented a vault in St. Louis Cemetery Number One. He went and stuffed a man in that dark space, taping off his mouth so no one would hear him scream too much. Paid the workers to seal the boy right up, they say."

That was mean, all right. "What did someone do to deserve that?"

"He was a college kid who tried to cheat Damien in the game of twenty-one. But that's nothing, Waller. My boss likes to drive people to the swamps, where he feeds the creepies a main course of Man Jambalaya."

Waller could just feel his own skin getting gnawed by imaginary chompers. But he'd come against tough subjects before, especially while working the crime beat. There was the rapist in New York whom Waller had helped catch back in the early eighties. He'd tracked the bastard to a woman's home, where the creep had imitated a cat outside her window to lure her out. Luckily, Waller had intervened, but not before the man had cut Waller's arm with a knife.

Still, it was a scar he wore proudly. But there were other wounds, more mental than physical—beaten children and wives, tortured murder victims.

Waller turned all that off, especially since Roxy was watching him, gauging him with those sad eyes.

"Do *you* feel safe with Theroux?" he asked, his voice lowered.

"Aw, yeah. He trusts me enough. But I'll be certain never to ask questions or step on his tail."

Relief flooded Waller. If the guy *ever* laid a hand on Roxy, he'd…

She was talking again. "He's mostly levelheaded. Mostly. Damien certainly knows how to run his businesses, I tell you. Why, his gaming room alone…"

As if she'd said too much, she pursed her lips and let go of Waller's hand. Instinctively, he grabbed for hers, missing the warmth of the contact.

But she'd already stepped back.

"Gaming room?" Waller asked, unable to help himself.

"Why you asking? You a gamer?"

"I suppose. I like some poker every now and again."

She considered him. "Damien runs a good room. Better than anyone in the city. The only problem comes when a fellow tries to cheat him."

God, if he could gain entrance...

"I bluff well," he said, trying to convince her he was worthy, "but other than that, I try to be honest."

At that, Roxy seemed to come to a decision. After glancing around, she disappeared for a moment. While she was gone, Waller tried to still his excitement, the thrill of the big race to come.

When she returned, she slipped him a crystal token with a panther etched into it, gave him directions to a place called Club Lotus and instructed him on how to use the marker for entrance.

"It won't be open again for a few more days, so if you've got the bug for poker, go tonight," she said. "Damien could use more good customers like you."

"Thanks. You're a man's best friend."

"That's what they all say."

After tossing that comment his way, Roxy wandered off to wait on other customers. What did she mean exactly? Did she have a lot of boyfriends? What kind of man did she date?

Was Waller even her type?

As his mind turned over these questions, he inspected the crystal marker, knowing he'd damned well use it.

And, hours later, when he did, he understood what Roxy had been telling him about Damien Theroux's temper.

THE FOLLOWING NIGHT AT TWO o'clock, Damien drove his Galaxie around the Quarter with a blindfolded woman in the passenger seat.

Gem. The next journalist on his list of people to fool.

He glanced at her again as the street lamps bathed her in passing illumination. Wisps of her light hair brushed against the silk material covering her eyes. She clutched a handle on the door, fisted her other hand in her lap.

Clearly, she hadn't expected this when he'd promised to show her his "world." Hadn't expected her teasing, fantasy flirtations to translate into something far more serious.

Earlier, after she'd reported to work, Damien had asked her to meet him in his office after hours. Then he'd brought out the blindfold, capturing her sense of sight while he whispered naughty promises in her ear and drove her to Dante's Basement.

A "sex club" that would be in business for this night only.

Though the house he was using—another property he owned—wasn't far from Cuffs, Damien wanted her to think the location was far away, ultrasecret. A danger to anyone who could reveal its whereabouts.

So, as he finally pulled to the curb on Dauphine Street and cut the engine, he left her blinded, helpless.

Without a word, he got out of the car, went around to her side and guided her out. Just the smoothness of her hand against his was enough to stir up the never-ending lust in his mind, the ache in his groin. As he shut

Gem's door and turned her to face the front of his property, he caught a whiff of her lemony perfume.

Once again, his body clutched in on itself. Needing. Keening to be inside of her.

And he intended to be tonight.

"Are we here?" she asked, moving as if to take off the eye cover. She was breathless, maybe even a little too afraid for such a big-girl reporter.

Though something feeble in him wanted to hold her safe—useless, that emotion—Damien would nevertheless manipulate her. He had no choice in the matter.

Vising her wrist in his grip, he stopped her from removing the blindfold. "Wait," he said, soft and low. "You're here by my pleasure, Gem, and I don't want you to find your way back."

He glanced up at the slim four-story house, its wooden facade painted in baby-blue with navy shutters. Iron chairs, barely visible through the white wooden railing, rested on the galleries. The windows were naked, curtainless. Damien had ordered the lace removed for now, knowing that the street withstood frequent traffic and faced a popular hotel across the way.

Gem would soon find out why this would matter.

As he led her inside, a song by Edith Piaf floated through the incense-laced air. The French lyrics added to the exotic atmosphere he'd wanted to create in Gem's mind. Little would she know that this downstairs floor was furnished with a time-faded chandelier, musty velvet couches and scarred walnut tables.

A former hotel parlor.

An abandoned building—not a sex club.

So many lies he was going to tell to her so he could survive, Damien thought. Just like last night, when he'd put on quite a show for Waller Smith.

He positioned Gem by the staircase, then stepped back to appreciate her—tumbled blond hair losing its starlet upsweep, a long neck made for caresses. His caresses alone, he thought.

Breasts pushing at her black tank, the small, firm mounds of them peeking over the low collar of her shirt. Skirt brushing toned, tanned legs made longer by those sexy pumps with the straps around her ankles.

He wanted to get his fill of her before the corruption began. Before her punishment and his deception kicked into gear.

He almost regretted having to do this.

"I'm going to take you upstairs," he said, knowing the professionals that Kumbar had hired were ready to go. "But I'm not going to let you see everything yet, Gem. I know you like to listen. I know it excites you."

A smile lifted her mouth. Brave. A screw-you sign that he wasn't scaring her.

"Then bring it on," she said.

He waited until they heard the first flick of the whip from a room on the next floor. At the crack of it, she flinched, rested her hand on the wooden stair rail.

"Dante's Basement is up the steps." He moved forward. "I'm eager to see which room you like in particular."

Quick breathing was making her chest rise and fall, but she lifted her foot toward the stairs, felt around for that first riser.

A blast of desire lit him up. She was game, his brave waitress. They would have quite a time tonight if she stayed so open to the possibilities.

Walking in back of her, Damien made sure she didn't waver, didn't stumble. When they got to the landing, another snap of the whip sang over the civilized, romantic music of the parlor. From the room opposite, a man cried out, begging an unseen partner for more. The only response was female laughter—wicked and knowing.

Acting, Damien knew.

But even as he thought it, he guessed that Kumbar— the man who'd arranged all this—was in a locked room at the end of the hall with Kandi, passing time or whatever they liked to call it, while Damien taught Gem her lessons.

And why not, Damien thought. Last night had been a rough one, with them staging that *other* scene for Waller Smith's sake.

When Roxy had called from Cuffs to let him know the reporter had taken her bait, Damien had not only cringed inwardly at the self-derision of her tone, but had entertained a moment of hesitation. Yes, another one. But that hadn't stopped him from supervising as Kumbar and Jean roughed up one of the Dulac family's men who'd volunteered to slump in a chair and take a few blows. The junior mob member had been paid a nice bonus for getting slapped around by Jean.

Sadly, with a sense of childhood lost, Damien had noted the emergence of crime-boss steel in his good friend as he'd pretended to punish the "cheater." But, still, he'd ignored the pangs of remorse, carrying on with his plan for the reporter.

The whole time, they'd known Waller Smith was watching. Damien's trusted employees had made sure the journalist had found himself a proper spy seat near the grating that led to the room off an alley.

But now it was out of Damien's hands and up to the reporter to make Theroux the revered figure he once was in this town.

The whip popped again, and a groan split the air, bringing Damien back to the moment. Gem pivoted on her heel, hand out, blindly seeking him.

His heart gave a twist, as if it'd too suddenly turned direction. Without thinking, he accepted her hand, held her palm to his chest, offering comfort he couldn't afford to give.

"Scared?" he asked, slowly taking her touch away.

Her mouth quirked, as if to say, *Don't you wish.*

Then she moved to the opposite door, where the man was still begging his woman for "more." What that was, not even Damien was sure about.

Here, Gem leaned her head against the frame. She looked lost, tired in a way that most people get when they're torn.

Did she regret crossing him? Or was that wishful dreaming on his part?

He put his back to the opposite wall, crossing one ankle over the other and barring his arms over his chest as the next two rooms down the hall went into action. Additional groans, cries, fervent demands.

"Damien, what exactly is going on?"

A reporter's question, merely solidifying what was obvious. He wondered which room would be her undoing, when the symphony of insinuations would get to her.

If, in a moment of complete abandon, she would confess to him.

Fat chance.

"I'm sure you know," he said, watching as she traced a hand over the wood of the door. "This is an exclusive club for people with particular tastes. Tastes like yours."

She laughed. "I don't think so."

Nervous? Had he been wrong about her level of experience?

"Yes, you do." He moved away from the wall. "You think a lot of the time, don't you? You think and think, and when you believe no one else is watching, you go deeper. You imagine things you'd never tell anyone about. Things good girls like Gem James would never do."

Another step closer. She lifted her face toward him, and he knew he was right. Then she turned the rest of her body away from the door, her back to the wall—inviting him.

He took the summons most gladly, bracing his hands above her head and pressing his full body to hers, stretching his length along those legs, her hips, her breasts. His awakening cock nuzzled her softest spot as he rubbed himself downward, teasing her.

In answer, she shifted her hips, making room for him, letting out a soft mewl of delight. Though he wanted to see the passion in her eyes, he was afraid to take off that blindfold, just in case her gaze reflected something he didn't dare acknowledge in himself.

Against her heat, he allowed his hard-on to grow.

"Tell me your most secret fantasy, Gem. Tell me what sort of room you want to be in, and I'll make it come true."

Restlessly, she swiveled against him until he couldn't stand it anymore. With a protesting moan, he reached down with one hand and cupped her ass, grinding her against him.

She spoke between subtle thrusts. "I've...never lost...control. Never..."

Taking hold of his back, she rocked against him, pressed her face against his chest. Her words were moist against his shirt.

"Never...disappointed...anyone by...doing the wrong..." She gave a strained little cry. "...thing."

Damien, himself, was struggling for control. But he would be damned if he came with a round of dry humping.

Pinning her against the wall with one emphatic drive, he felt the beat of her blood against his erection. Or was that his own pounding body?

"Am I the wrong thing for you?" he asked, rasping out the words as they both remained in the same intimate position. "Am I a bad influence?"

"I'm...sure of it." She panted, scratching her fingernails up his chest while she regained some oxygen. "I'll never...let my guard down around you."

Then she grinned, making him think she might be joking. Even so, her words still had a bite to them.

When Damien screwed women, he didn't joke. It was pure business. He made them weep, made them claw for more, but it wasn't because he was a silver-tongued charmer.

Odd, how with Gem it wasn't that way. Part of their foreplay was banter, double entendres.

"So," she said, having gained composure, "if I let you pick a room, would I be able to trust your judgment? Could I be sure you're leading me into the right one?"

Damien allowed her to slide to the floor. A slow melt back down his body, like honey down his skin.

"Trust? I think if you're going to fulfill a fantasy, there's no trust allowed. You're the one who likes danger." He leaned down to her ear, breathed into it. "So trust me not to be trusted."

With that, he peeled her off the wall and walked her down the hall, the floorboards croaking under their weight. When he got to the final room—one with curtainless windows facing the well-lit Dauphine Inn—he let her in.

The hinges *ahhhh*ed like an audience on the edge of its seat.

And when he took off her blindfold, she blinked.

Then gasped.

9

At first the low lighting stung Gemma's eyes as the weight of her silk blindfold was lifted from her face. But everything else in the room stunned her even more.

Diaphanous burgundy material was draped above intricate, cathouse-type furniture. Flickering gas lanterns hung on the white, paint-chipped walls, creating shadows and voodoo. Uncurtained windows revealed the lights of a building across the street. In one window, a woman walked by, tilting her head while fastening an earring. In another, the colors of a television set flashed over a pair of bare feet propped on a table opposite it.

But the contents of this room *really* caught Gemma's attention.

She wandered to a table near the expansive mosquito-netted bed. Toys—from the tame to the imaginative. Velvet-lined handcuffs, dildos of all shapes and sizes, some sort of contraption that looked like an eggbeater.

What had she gotten herself into? Besides what she and Damien had started in the hall, that is.

Her body was still sizzling from the foreplay. Even

recalling it—arching hips, hot juices causing her to slide against the erection she'd encouraged—flipped Gemma's stomach, exciting her.

She chopped out a breath, turning away from the toy table, then wandered to an open armoire. There, sumptuous clothing—from leather to lace—peeked out. Just to still her nervous hands, she sifted through the costumes, extracting one and presenting it to Damien on its padded satin hanger.

"I've never seen *this* in the pages of *Vogue*."

He didn't even glance at the ensemble, a red satin corset with attached garters. Instead, he was focusing intently on her.

Was he imagining what she'd look like with it on?

With her breasts spilling over the top, her bottom bare and vulnerable to his touch?

A crop was attached to the hanger, too. Dominatrix couture.

"We can do better," he said, a ruthlessly erotic smile on his lips.

Men had never looked at Gemma this way before. Not with this intensity, eyes glowing like a beast in the night. Sex had always been so vanilla. No wonder she'd cultivated such a rich fantasy life as an alternative.

As he moved to the armoire, as well, Gemma's skin prickled with the awareness of closed distance, with the knowledge that she was lying to him with every breath. Even if she seemed in control of herself right now, she wasn't. Not with her blood thudding, her brain spinning.

Even if she didn't want to admit it, she'd found herself, hadn't she? Discovered an odd slant of need that had been buried under so many layers that it'd only existed in her mind. The few other men she'd been with hadn't touched this part of Gemma Duncan.

Swallowing hard, she brushed against Damien's arm as she explored the clothing with him. A silk French-maid uniform. A cheerleader outfit. A *Dangerous Liaisons*-era gown with a bodice designed to lift and expose the full chest of some chosen woman.

"Rather dramatic," she said, wondering which one would render him senseless. "Any pirate costumes in here? I'd really— Oh."

He was holding up a filmy blue peignoir. Its hem flowed to the floor, the front splitting open in anticipation of revealing the dainty panties connected to the hanger. Simple, elegant. She'd feel like a princess in something so beautiful.

"Put this on, *chérie*." His voice sounded like aged parchment, crumbling and ready to fall apart.

After she put the corset back in the armoire, he gave the peignoir to her, the sheer material catching a breeze from the ceiling fan like a ghost in flight.

The gown would hide nothing, but that's why she'd come here, right? So *her* exposure would encourage his own.

She took it from him, went to the bed, lay the peignoir down on the white silk comforter. First, she undid the straps of her shoes, peering over her shoulder to find that he'd turned his back to face the window.

Streetlights played over his body, soft yellow, as he braced his hands on either side of the frame. As she slipped out of her tank and skirt, she thought now might be a good time to get to work.

Unfortunately.

"How long has Dante's been in business?" she asked offhandedly.

He kept looking outside. "For a short time. The building was abandoned for a spell. It was a boutique hotel in the twenties, a place where movie stars and socialites used to stay when visiting the city. Now…"

He trailed off, not having to finish. Now it was a whorehouse. A den of warped dreams for those brave enough to enter.

Containing her anxiety, Gemma shrugged off her bra while inspecting the rest of the room. Red-tinged paintings featuring orgasmic women and nude bodies entwined with each other. Silken ropes attached to the bed's headboard. A washbowl on a table near the door.

It was filled with water and red petals, accompanied by a dish of soap and a thick hand towel. Stepping out of her underwear, she went to it.

Roses. She scooped up a palm full of water and trickled it over her body. Then, after using the soap, she repeated the luxurious rhythm. Moisture puddled on the planks around her bare feet, making the atmosphere carelessly primitive, wild.

Still looking out the window, Damien had his head cocked to the side, as if he was picturing the sheen of fresh dampness over her skin. Naughtiness piqued, she made a few languidly pleased sounds and finally dried herself with the fluffy little towel.

Then she went back to the peignoir, encasing herself

in sin. The bodice hugged her breasts, the smooth material causing her nipples to bead against it. The front slit fanned open to reveal her stomach, her almost see-through panties and a length of leg.

"You were saying…" She continued where he left off, just as if there hadn't been a sultry lull in conversation. "Now this building is a *house of ill repute,* as they would've called it."

So did that mean she was a prostitute of some sort? Was she selling her body for fame and prestige? In the process of giving herself something to be proud of, was she actually destroying what she had left of her dignity?

The thought stopped Gemma cold. Seconds ago, all she'd wanted to do was sneak up in back of him and ease off his shirt, turn him around so he could devour her with his gaze. Now, she couldn't bring herself to do it.

She'd gone too far—hadn't she?—by coming here.

He must have sensed the change in her, because he had faced her again, silhouetted by the window's light. After a long pause, he walked toward a pull rope in the corner of the room, tugged at it. Down the hall, in the midst of the moaning and whip cracking, she heard a chorus of bells.

"Gem…" He was bathing her with another endless gaze, seeing all of her for the first time. "You're more than I ever imagined." He paused. "How many men have loved you?"

The personal question startled her. She wanted to give him a count-on-two-hands number, to bluster and present herself as a real pro. But she was too rattled to lie this time.

"Three," she said, wanting to add a phrase like *pathetic, huh?* just to lighten the mood, to dig herself out of this sudden hole of revelation.

"Were you in love?" he asked.

She couldn't see his face; it was still tinted by darkness.

"I thought so. But...well...none of the men worked out." She tried to put on her tough act again. "Not that I'm any worse off for it."

"They came out the losers." He finally moved to her, his steps slow and sure.

"And you," she said. "I'll bet you've slept with half the city."

Why was she so damned nervous? Couldn't she stop her dumb comments from ruining the seduction, her interrogation?

He didn't answer, but then again, he didn't have to. His silence told Gemma how out of her league he was.

Now Damien was standing in front of her, all six feet plus of him. With practiced ease, he reached out, cupped both palms beneath her breasts like a man getting ready to quench a thirst.

Gemma flinched, stoked hot by the motion of his thumbs lightly rubbing over her nipples. Then, when he coasted his hands lower, she held her breath.

He sculpted her, memorizing her ribs, her waist, her belly, her hips and thighs. Then around to the back, where he trailed upward, over her rear, the small of her back.

There, he stopped, massaging, making her sway with every knead of his hands.

"Now we choose your room, Gem," he said.

With one last brush of his knuckle against her lower stomach, he led her to the door, opened it. Immediately, Gemma crossed her arms over her chest, shielding herself.

"No." A command. "At Dante's you don't hide. You don't hold back."

Check your innocence at the door.

Knowing full well that she'd chucked her so-called innocence right out of the solar system when she'd first pitched this assignment, Gemma uncovered herself. Then she shot Theroux an I'm-up-to-anything glance.

The breath rushed out of him, and his appreciation affected her, too, warming her. Making her feel beautiful.

He ushered her into the hallway.

Once outside, Gemma's adrenaline froze in her veins. Each door was now open, waiting for her. Men and women in all stages of dress lingered, smoking cigarettes, giving her the once-over. Inspecting the new girl.

Is that why he'd pulled the bell rope? To summon them?

Thoroughly aware that they could see through her peignoir, Gemma gave into the trap she'd set for herself with a shiver of ecstasy, then walked toward the stairs to the first door. To the one where the whip had sounded.

Murmurs of approval followed her and, for the first time in her life, Gemma realized that she was wearing her fantasies in public. And, incredibly, she wasn't ashamed of her skin, her naked need for something more than a normal let's-cook-spaghetti-and-stay-in-tonight man who didn't have a chance of fulfilling her.

A woman dressed in a black catsuit and half mask greeted her at door number one. She stretched a whip in her hands, flexing the leather. When Gemma peeked inside the room, she saw a man kneeling on the floor, hands on thighs, panting. Red welts glistened amidst the sweat on his back in the candlelight. He turned to Gemma, smiling.

O-kay. No door number one for her. But, my oh my, when she finally wrote this story, it was going to be a doozy.

"No?" Theroux asked, his voice challenging.

"No." Gemma turned to the opposite door, where, earlier, a man had been begging for "more." Inside, there was a spread of food over silk-clothed tables. Frostings, sauces, all manner of culinary yum-yums.

The food-fetish alcove? Could be her thing.

Or maybe not. When Gemma spied a man and a woman reclining on the bed, she noticed that the guy had a combination of whipped cream and…was it wax?…dripped over his chest. Next to him, the underwear-clad female toyed with the stem of a candle.

Yeah, that was definitely wax on his chest.

"The body-palate room," Damien said.

As quickly as she could, Gemma moved next door.

"Not your style?" he asked.

This time, Gemma turned around to gauge him. Yup, amused as ever. "Does it pull *your* trigger?"

"Depends on my mood." He slid a finger under her

chin, caressed it. "Dante's takes reservations in advance, so if you don't find what you like tonight, there are more rooms to come."

With growing assurance, she'd already decided which room she liked the best. The one with Theroux in it. The one where they could be alone, creating their own turn-ons.

But she let him continue the tour.

He brought her to the next room and the next, as if thinking she wanted something kinkier than just body-to-body contact with him tonight.

And why wouldn't he? She'd told him she did.

Was it true? What exactly *was* she looking for?

There was a room that seemed as if it catered to group sex because of all the shiny, oiled people lounging around on the harem pillows. A room where men and women smoked hookah pipes while sitting on cushions in a voyeuristic circle around a plush feather mattress. A room opposite their original one, where a woman and man stood outside, draped over each other.

They were dressed like a belly dancer and a sultan, their costumes falling off their shoulders, as if they'd been put on hastily.

As Gemma looked closer, the couple seemed familiar. The man, with his dark skin, stocky build and tight, closely cropped curls. The woman, with a complexion like cocoa and hair like a black cloud.

It would be stupid to ask if she knew them. What if she'd met them while doing her reporting? That'd pretty much blow her cover.

Instead, she asked, "Any pirate costumes in there?"

The man looked to Theroux, shrugged, then took his lady back inside the room.

Gemma turned to Damien. "I wouldn't mind pirates."

"I'll work on that. But for now, what's your choice?"

Before she answered, she realized where she'd seen that last couple before. At Cuffs. They'd been the ones who'd gone upstairs for sex. Looooong, second-floor, years-in-the-process sex.

Was Cuffs a Dante's annex? Did they use the rooms when the Basement was too crowded?

Gemma gestured to the last room, the one they'd been in earlier. "What's the theme here?"

When Theroux answered, he seemed to peer into her, to read every desire, every vein of longing that held her together.

"It can be anything you make it, Gem."

As everyone returned to their posts and shut the doors, a slight wind huffed down the hallway, into their room, making the lanterns dance with disturbed light.

Tentatively, she took his hand in hers, then pulled him inside. He shut the door behind him.

"What do you want it to be?" he asked softly.

The sex-shop objects on the table entered her mind, but toys didn't appeal. She wanted...

A bad boy. A bad situation.

He seemed to know. But hadn't that been the case all along? Wasn't that why she was here with him, ignoring those nice-girl lessons of her life and chancing everything for a man who would hate her eventually?

With the confidence of a predator that frequently

lures prey into its trap, he reeled her in, maneuvered her in front of the window, her back to his chest.

The woman who'd been putting on an earring was arguing with her husband. They were so close that Gemma could read their lips and hear their voices through the gaping window. They were debating about whether they should stay up all night listening to jazz or just get some shut-eye for their airboat swamp tour tomorrow. In the other window, the couple who'd been watching TV were toasting each other with champagne—some cheap generic brand—and opening the window to the thick night air.

"Can they see us?" she asked on a breath, already suspecting the answer.

Damien splayed his hands over her ribs, ran them downward, resting them over her bared belly, rubbing circles into her skin with the pads of his fingers.

"There's enough light so they can see what we're doing, yes. Will that stop you?"

Dragonflies winged through her stomach, moving lower, flapping electric wings against her clit, making her restless. "No."

"Très bien."

He kissed the side of her neck, nipping at a throbbing vein, causing her to lean into the contact. At the same time, she kept an eye on the people across the street, hoping they would go about their business and ignore this wicked behavior.

Hoping they would look.

His fingers moved downward, skimming into her panties, sliding between the swollen folds of her sex.

He surrounded her tender nub, worked it until she rested her weight back against him.

By now, the champagne swillers were leaning out the window, toasting each car that drove down the street. The other couple had split apart, leaving only the man in the window, still debating with his unseen wife.

Damien's breath was coming faster in her ear. "Tonight I'll slip right into you. How long can you wait for it?"

Cocky jerk. "Forever."

With that, he laughed, then urged a finger up inside of her, swirling it around. "Then I'll make sure it takes that long."

She was barely holding it together, her body in flux, like a pan of paint being sloshed back and forth, mingling in color and texture.

"Just try," she managed. "Try to outlast me, Damien."

"I will."

He inserted a second finger into her, thrusting upward so that his thumb pressed against her clit. Groaning, Gemma fell against the window, head cradled against an arm, breasts crushed against the glass. Her hardened nipples glided up and down against the slippery cool of it, moving with his every demand.

Then, unable to help herself, she parted her braced arms, looking between them, keeping their maybe-audience in sight. Her heart beat double time at the thought of getting caught.

It was a lot like that college party. Danger.

"You've been an easy touch in the past," he said, his whisper ragged. "You'll cream in another minute."

Now this was more than sex. It was her showing him that she would get her man. That she would exceed expectation and never fail herself again.

Gemma reached in back of her, sketching over his rock-hard crotch. "I give *you* thirty seconds."

That did it. He abandoned her nether regions and used both hands to grasp the straps of her peignoir. With a rough tug, he tore it off her, the material screeching.

The air licked at her exposed skin.

Wasting no time, he yanked off her panties, too, but she was already whipping around, grabbing his shirt and ripping. Buttons flew, hitting the wall, the floor.

In response, he buried a hand in her hair, and she thought, *This is it. The kiss.*

But he didn't make a move.

Instead, they both tested each other with rapacious glares.

A world of difference spanned the short distance between them. As she measured the depths of his pale eyes, she discovered a deep well of hurt in the center of them.

Why was he watching her like this?

In that moment, she wanted to know everything about him: What he'd been like as a kid. Where his family lived. Why he'd turned to crime. Whether he'd ever been in love.

Slowly, she raised herself up, sweeping the tips of her breasts over his smooth, muscled chest.

A kiss. Just a kiss.

For a moment, his gaze softened and his lips parted as he bent to meet her.

A jagged whisper separated them.

But then he jerked, just slightly. Froze.

A beat passed, like the ticking of a bomb—infinite and nerve shattering.

Then something in the pale of his eyes expanded. Released.

He spun her around again, bringing her back to the window—as if he couldn't stand to face her. To touch lips. To let her in.

"Let's get their attention," he said, referring to the embattled husband and the tipsy couple. Ignoring what had almost just happened between them. "Let's give a show."

As she hugged the wooden frame again, Damien pulled off the rest of his shirt. Then he did away with all his clothing, taking care to fix a rubber over his hard-on.

Naked, he pressed himself to her, skin covering sweat-dabbed skin. Of its own volition, his cock nudged between her thighs, seeking the wetness, the plumped readiness.

As she whimpered, spreading her legs and wiggling her hips backward to allow the tip of him to slide against her, guilt stretched his pores. The feeling was as heavy as the humidity, shrouding him.

He couldn't kiss her. He never kissed women, never saw the point in it. The act was only a means to an end— the end being this, what they already had now.

Explosive sex. Orgasm.

Kissing didn't get you the thrill of either of them, so why do it?

He wouldn't admit to avoiding something deeper.

Innocence. The regaining of it with such a tender touch.

Damn Gem for reminding him.

He spoke with undue harshness. "What would your friends think if they were watching? What would all those people who thought you were a responsible girl say to you?"

He hated himself for doing this, for trying to punish her because she'd hurt him with her betrayal.

"Just touch me, Damien." Her words sounded bruised.

He'd pushed a button, hadn't he?

Teasing her with the tip of his penis, he laughed, his fingers reaching beneath the firm smoothness of her rear to open her folds wider. "What will these people across the street say to their own friends about the couple they saw screwing like animals?"

"I'm sure it'll get a good laugh or two. Please, Damien."

So, she couldn't stand the wait. Hell, he couldn't, either. The center of him was hammering, taking him over. Moisture had even started to seep out of him and gather in the top of the rubber.

Beaten, Damien raised his arms and folded them over her own, plastering his damp skin against hers. In a moment of utter weakness, he allowed himself to nest his face into her lemon-breeze hair, to breathe her in and keep her for only a few seconds.

Then, on a hitched curse, he slid into her with one deep drive, careful to avoid breaking the glass. Gemma pressed forward, face so close to the window that her breath steamed the panes, clouding them like a disappearing heartbeat that only reappeared, time and again, to fade away.

"There…" she sighed.

She was tight, so damned tight and nice, surrounding him like one of the velvet cuffs on the nearby table. Capturing him. Never letting go.

In, out, in…

Without thinking, he felt his fingers entwine with hers as they both palmed the window frame.

Through the haze of his sight, he saw the man across the way make a bitter gesture at his wife, then turn toward the window. He stopped in his steps, mouth agape as he squinted and crept closer to his picture-box view.

Gemma gasped, and by instinct, Damien moved her sideways toward the cover of the armoire, so that they were out of the man's sight. Freakin' pervert.

"But…" she said.

"No, you belong to me." And he meant it…for the moment.

A long, satisfied "mmm" escaped her as she collapsed against the armoire, hugging the old, polished wood. It was the sound of a woman who wanted something more than what was happening now.

His blood quickened, and he nuzzled a hand over her sex, giving him leverage and allowing her to bend forward slightly to accommodate his slick pounding. The gentle ramming that was coming faster…faster.

At the same time, his fingers played her, made her cry out, asking for more.

But this was all he could give, he thought, riding her, thrusting and swaying with the music of a jazz song gone awry.

Wet skin, sliding and skimming. A saxophone dripping notes in slow time.

Warm fluids, coating thighs and sensitive flesh. A bass raining the blues.

His hips, grinding, bringing them both to a crescendo. Drums, pounding out a crazed beat with no sense or rhythm.

Louder, faster, different scales losing their structure and falling like beads from a balcony.

Harder, and harder still, circles of color shattering on the streets and bursting upward, burning whoever was standing in their way.

As he exploded into the condom, she rocked forward, clutching the armoire for balance. Then, as he caught his breath—his emotions—she glanced over her shoulder.

He knew she wasn't done.

For the second time in days, he went down on his knees for a woman, finally turning her toward him. He brought Gem to her own flash of contentment with his mouth, loving the act of loving her.

Wishing he could somehow make it more.

When she was done, the taste of her still on his tongue, she smoothed his hair with tender hands, relaxed back against the armoire and tilted her face upward.

In a raw whisper, she said, "Believe it or not, Damien Theroux, I know more about you because of sex than anything else. Especially now."

He didn't know exactly what she meant, but he suspected that he'd given away too much with his body.

And, oddly enough, he wasn't all that sorry.

Not until they'd made love again on the bed, and he'd blindfolded and driven her home—or rather, back to her designated Garden District corner—for the night.

Then he was plenty sorry.

10

BACK IN *WEEKLY GOSSIP* LAND, Gemma tried her best to get something done.

She'd had two days off from Cuffs. A vacuum of time she'd tried to fill by finding every lame excuse in the book to claw her way back to see Damien. Touch Damien. God, if she could even just catch a hint of his scent, that'd be enough.

Now, as she found herself back in her editor's office, Gemma fought a useless inner battle—sex drive versus career survival. Deathmatch 2005.

Your body's just a little overwhelmed, she told herself during her more lucid moments. *You're still in the throes of first-sex estrogen rampage. It'll be over soon, don't worry.*

"Gemma?"

It was Nancy Mendoza, leaning back in her all-purpose General chair and giving her reporter the what's-with-you? eye. Her prim bun, white button-down and linen skirt reminded Gemma of what she used to be herself.

A straight-and-narrow career girl.

"I'm just tired," Gemma said, flopping into the chair

in front of Nancy's desk. "Two jobs can suck the life out of you. Not that I'm whining."

"Good. I can't abide crybabies." Nancy grinned and leaned forward, still giving her the once-over. "You wanted to see me about something?"

The editor had been out of town visiting relatives for a long weekend, so this was the first chance Gemma had to tell her about Dante's. "You won't believe what I found."

And she described the hedonistic Basement and the leads about Theroux's criminal activities. The certainty that there was a lot more than he was telling her.

"So," Nancy said, nodding with satisfaction, "this undercover gig is really working."

"Really well. In fact, I know things about Theroux that no one else could guess at."

True. After their intimate encounter, she knew he liked to keep himself guarded—even from his lovers. Knew that he'd fought to avoid kissing her and getting too close. Knew that he was capable of tearing her right down the middle without even trying.

After what they'd done, she didn't know if her heart was in the story anymore. All that mattered was a kiss.

One kiss.

There'd been a stretch of time when she'd actually convinced herself that he was opening up to her. That it would only be a matter of time before he cupped her face in his hands and kissed her until they melded together.

But then he'd driven her back to the Garden District, and she'd seen the change come over him as soon as she'd gotten out of the car. All tenderness had disappeared, taken over by his typical rough arrogance.

"Don't be late for work Wednesday," he'd told her in parting, then driven away.

No, "When can I see you again?" or "I adore you, Gem." Not that she expected him to fall for her, but...

Well, maybe she wished it.

"You know," Nancy said, "for a while I thought I might have to take you off of this story, that maybe you were starting to develop some feelings for Theroux. I wondered about your journalistic distance."

Distance. Gemma cleared her throat and tried not to blush. There wasn't a whole lot of distance between her and her subject now. Yet she wasn't about to jeopardize her career by confessing her methods of obtaining information. Absolutely no way.

Sex was fleeting. Careers lasted longer.

The justification fell apart even as she thought about it.

"You'll get your ink," Gemma said, wishing she could confide in Nancy as she had before this weekend. Talk about distance, there was a lot of it between editor and reporter right now.

Gemma missed her budding friendship with Nancy. Missed the camaraderie of simply hanging out and having fun with this other woman. The price of success.

Her friend stared at her for a moment, and Gemma had the feeling she was thinking the same thing.

But then Nancy blinked, smiled faintly and shuffled some papers. Editor mode. "I'll tell you what. Since things are getting interesting with Theroux, you've got an additional week to get dirt on him, and I'll assign another reporter to the local-color desk for that time."

"Really?" Gemma jumped out of her seat. "Oh, Nancy, thank you. This calls for us to go out to dinner. Soon."

"Sounds like a plan. But—"

"Be careful," Gemma finished for her.

She was interrupted by one of her ringing cell phones; Gemma carried two—one belonging to "Gem," and one for personal use. Nancy relaxed in her chair, shooing her out of the office at the same time.

Waving, Gemma left and flipped open her personal phone to find a strange number lighting her screen. She headed for the lounge while answering.

"Hello?"

"Gemma Duncan?" A muddled voice, male.

Entering the lounge, she took a quick peek around and decided it was empty except for the humming soda machine and the drip of a sink's faucet that needed fixing.

"This is Gemma. Who is this?"

"An anonymous source. I hear you're working on a piece about Damien Theroux."

Gemma's heart bolted, zipping upward like a scared cat clawing up a curtain. "How—"

"It doesn't matter how I know. And I'm calling from a pay phone, so don't bother tracing this. You might want to check into these names—Venus's Fly, Bacchanal and Mojo."

Gemma whipped out the pen and notepad she kept in her pockets when in the office. She wrote down the tips.

"Why are these important?"

"Prostitution," said the voice. "Services that'll provide men and women for gaming clients."

"Where are they located?"

He gave her the addresses, each in the Quarter. But when she pursued his identity again, the line went dead.

Damn. She checked her phone, called the number back, but it merely rang and rang.

She barely noticed Waller Smith cruising into the lounge to access the soda machine. The thud of the aluminum can hurling itself out of the purchase chute startled her, causing her to clutch her notes to her chest.

"Morning, Duncan," he said, popping open his drink.

There was nothing scruffy about Smith today. Actually, when Gemma thought about it, his bleary edges had started to disappear little by little this past week. First, with the introduction of better shirts. Second, with eyes that weren't quite as red anymore. And what had happened to all those naps? She hadn't seen him snoozing for days. As a matter of fact, every time she passed his desk, he was on the phone or typing away like a demon.

"Hi, Smith," she said, still wary.

He strolled nearer. "What're you hiding? The ultimate ammunition against your friend and mine?"

She tucked the notes into her skirt's pocket. "This? Hardly. I'm still at square one with Theroux."

Smith took a sip, regarding her over the top of the can, then said, "That's not what I gather."

Okay, thought Gemma, *it's stupid to lie to him. He's been around Cuffs. He's seen what's going on.*

Done with waiting for her to answer, Smith barged ahead. "Listen, I know some crap about Theroux that isn't real romantic, so you might want to back off while there's still some backing to be done."

"And leave him all to you? Doubtful."

"Believe it or not, I'm not looking out for myself here." He really seemed concerned, taking a step forward and resting a hand on her arm. "I'm not kidding."

Gemma wilted, half sitting against the back of a lounge couch. She hadn't wanted to believe the mounting clues about Theroux. Hadn't wanted to admit that, maybe, there was no chance of him ever being a good guy after all.

But, still, something Jerome Lamont had said last week niggled at her.

Wouldn't the public love to know about these other dealings? Your weaknesses?

What are you, Theroux? Some self-appointed avenger?

What was it that was bothering her? And why wasn't she getting to the bottom of it?

Heaviness settled in her chest. "I've found out a few unsavory nuggets about Theroux, too."

And she'd been a part of those unscrupulous dealings.

"So you already know." Smith sunk to a seat next to her, the back of the couch holding both of their weight. "I'll tell you, how he treats his enemies... I haven't seen anything so brutal for years. And here I thought I'd gotten away from that when I turned to the tabloids."

Gemma kept her tongue, hoping he'd spill some more.

Sure enough, Smith was out to unburden his soul, though she couldn't believe he'd picked her to do it with.

Maybe it was because he knew she could relate?

"Duncan, Theroux and his cronies kicked the tar out of some poor guy who was cheating in the gaming room. I checked, and one of the toughs was Jean Dulac."

She knew the name from her research. Son of a local boss. But he and Damien had been connected in news stories before, so she wasn't surprised. What stunned her was Damien's part in the violence.

"What I don't understand," she said, voice soft, "is how he can be in this line of work. Face-to-face, he doesn't seem so terrible."

Smith actually flushed at her face-to-face reference, the universal code for hot sex, obviously. Yeah, he definitely suspected the worst of her. And, perversely, she was only too happy to confirm his worries.

Smith guzzled more soda, let out a long *ahhhh*. Then said, "Even Hannibal Lecter has his charms, Gemma. The best bad people succeed because there's always a saving grace about them, something that makes people want to give them a second chance. Just remember this—beneath it all, they're not like us. And as a reporter, you've got to stay frosty if you want to stay sane."

A ticker tape of office rumor ran through her head—people talking about Smith's former crack crime reporting. Black-and-white photos of front-page blood and death.

Suddenly, the thought of her co-worker's naps and

his lackadaisical attitude made sense. Had the never-ending human destruction exhausted him?

He started to wander out of the room.

"Smith?"

"Hmm?"

Gemma couldn't believe what she was about to ask. "Maybe, one day, would you mind sitting down and getting lunch with me, or something?"

He looked as shocked as she felt. But all she wanted was to hear a little of what he'd seen and done. What she could learn from him.

He nodded, shrugged. "We could do that."

Then, while fighting a grin, he left the room, leaving Gemma more optimistic, too. Might as well make your enemies your friends, right?

And, with his advice dominating her thoughts, she returned to her desk. Checked out the anonymous tipster's number—which was definitely a pay phone. Checked out the addresses—which were all abandoned buildings that could very well house criminal activity by night.

She'd get to the bottom of who owned them.

But just as she was about to, she got another call, this time from Roxy on the phone that belonged to "Gem." From home, the head waitress was calling to see if Gemma could cover for another waitress tonight.

After a pause which was sufficient enough for Gemma to do a mini Snoopy dance on her end of the line, she told Roxy that she thought she'd be able to make it.

THAT EVENING, AS WALLER held a single, perfect daisy in one hand and munched on a po'boy with help from the other, he leaned against the brick wall of Burgundy Grocery across from Cuffs and watched as Gemma reported for work.

What a kid. What could she want from a lunch with him? Probably some sort of mentor thing he'd suck at. Young reporters often leeched on to the older ones, thinking they'd absorb wisdom. Waller had seen it happen a thousand times. Not to him, though. Not lately, at least.

Duncan's invitation made him feel decent. Accepted into a club where he'd always been peeking in the window.

Still, he wasn't so flattered that he couldn't be honest with her. If she really wanted some advice, the first thing he'd repeat to her would be to get the hell away from Theroux. Even Roxy had been making under-the-breath comments lately about how her boss was losing it. Maybe she'd thought Waller couldn't hear, but, then again, he was excellent at reading those lips.

His younger sis in Ohio—deaf since she was five—could tell anyone that. Maybe it was time to visit her. They hadn't talked in years, though she kept sending unanswered Christmas and birthday cards to him.

Yeah. It was time to turn over that new leaf. And now might be a nice chance to do it.

He watched a few cars pass by while waiting for Roxy to stroll into her workplace. Okay, maybe he'd do his changing tomorrow. But right now he could at least plan. "Waller's Fresh Start." Good headline.

Still waiting, he composed a long mental checklist that became overwhelming within the first minute.

Would his new life mean that he should be efficient? Should he have his ear to a cell phone right now, tracking down other men who'd been messed over by Theroux?

Nah. Waller had been working that angle all day, and he needed a rest. He missed his naps sometimes.

But sleeping wouldn't have allowed him yet another good work day. Thanks to Roxy's loose lips, he'd located several sources to back up what he'd witnessed Theroux and his men do in that alley near Club Lotus. Even now, Waller could see the victim's head snap back with every smack, could feel all the bruises, could taste the tang of blood from the cuts on the poor sap's lips.

As he trashed the remnants of dinner and returned to his position against the wall—just like a fly, he thought, taking it all in—Roxy finally strolled down the street.

Her walk had an inner rhythm, as if she was listening to an Ella Fitzgerald tune and interpreting it with her hips. It was just one of the things he adored about her.

Waller clutched the lone daisy in his hand and made his way across the road to intercept her.

"Evening," he said, drawing himself up straight.

Her face lit up. Then, as if checking herself, she composed her delicate features. "We can always depend on you to be a regular, Waller. Why don't you come in?"

"I…" Not knowing what else to do, he presented the daisy. Its petals shook in the dusk's breeze. "I remember you said something about liking these."

For a minute, Waller thought Roxy was going to cry as she stared at the flower.

"Dammit," she said, voice quivery. "Why do you have to be so sweet?"

It sounded like an accusation but, for all the world, Waller wasn't sure what he could've done to make her angry.

"Take it," he said, seizing her hand and tangling her fingers around the stem. "It was growing in the backyard."

Actually, in someone else's backyard, since Waller didn't have one at his apartment. When he'd seen the flower while walking over here tonight, he'd thought of how Roxy had expressed a longing for one sunny flower that would tell her the world was still a good place. Even though he'd had to brave the curious stares of two porch-bound Maltese dogs while plucking Roxy's gift from a stranger's property, it'd been worth the trouble.

"Waller, you shouldn't have."

When she glanced up again, he could see that there was a tear running down her cheek. His heart cracked.

Without thinking twice, he reached out to thumb the moisture away. Roxy's eyes went wide. Then, hesitantly, she met his hand, wrapped her fingers around it, not seeming to mind his permanently ink-stained skin.

"I don't recall the last time someone remembered that I have a liking for daisies," she said. "It's akin to a person saying they like two lumps of sugar in their tea, or extra powered sugar on a beignet."

"I thought it was important," Waller said.

"And that's why I'm so fond of you."

Another tear rolled downward. It bathed the side of his hand, washing away everything else but the two of them.

"I wonder," she said, smiling a little, "how you like your beignets."

The hopeful side of him wished she was asking because she wanted to serve the donutlike treat to him some morning. In bed.

He cleared his throat. "Smothered with white stuff. That's how I take my breakfasts."

"Some night at Cuffs, I'll bring you a plateful," she said, smashing his fantasy. "I make a mean beignet."

"I'll bet." He rubbed his thumb against her fingers.

She sighed, nuzzled her sorrow-stained cheek against his hand. "I used to think that's what I was gonna do, you know. Have my own beignet shop. But then things went to hell in a handbasket with my marriage, and life changed. Cuffs came along and... You know."

Sure, he knew how that went. There used to be a time when Waller would envision his name on the cover of bestselling books that would save the world. "Why can't you still hope for that shop, Roxy?"

She gave a small laugh. "Because there ain't enough daisies in the world, if you know what I mean. But I like Cuffs well enough."

At that, she looked away, but Waller wasn't about to let her escape.

If he had any guts left in him, he'd show her how much he'd come to care for her. He'd make her feel as good about herself as she was doing to him. Because that was what affection was about, right? Bringing the other person up when they were down. Supporting them at all costs.

"Roxy?" he said softly.

She glanced up with those sad eyes, and he knew it was time to turn over that leaf he'd been thinking about.

With care, he bent down, lightly touched his mouth to hers, testing, wondering if she'd reject him or…

Gasping, she parted her lips slightly, accepting him.

She was soft, smelled so good—like cinnamon and sugar. When he brought his free hand to the back of her head, tangling his fingers into her silky red hair, Waller could just see that leaf turning, changing from the ugly underside to the smooth, bright face of a new future. His stomach echoed the rotation, going silly with longing.

Even though the kiss was gentle, the tickling flutter of a wing, it was the most powerful contact on earth. It shook him, making him remember all the first times of his life, all the dreams he'd hatched and watched die.

All the times he should've embraced what he wanted.

As she came up for air, leaning her forehead against his cheek and brushing his skin with her eyelashes, Roxy clutched at his arm. Waller caught her around the waist, keeping her upright as she used him for support.

"It's been a long time," she said.

"Yeah." The admission pained him. "Me, too."

They didn't say anything for a while, just clung to each other, with Roxy tucking her face against his shoulder and Waller closing his eyes, never wanting this to end.

But it did when someone next to them whispered, "Er…Roxy?"

Roxy bolted away from him, and Waller just stood there, arms empty and aching.

"Luc," she said, flapping a hand in front of her pink-ened face. "Good to see you."

The man, short and thick around the middle with thinning black hair and blue, puppy-dog eyes, adjusted the coat of his seemingly new suit. Sweat stains had marked the gray polyester near the armpits.

"Sorry 'bout that, Roxy," Luc said, sounding as if he'd been at the whiskey till very recently. "But you two're standin' in fronta the door."

Was that panic flashing over her face?

"You're going into Cuffs?" she asked. "Damien's not here right now."

True. Waller had seen him leave earlier.

Good ol' Luc wobbled to the side, righting himself before Waller could help.

"Jez stoppin' by to thank him." Suddenly, Luc's eyes welled up, his shoulders hunched forward, his face screwed into an emotional mess. "Than' God for Damien."

"Oh, Luc."

While Roxy shot Waller an anxious glance and took the man into a hug, Waller himself wondered why everyone was crying tonight.

The man embraced Roxy back, and Waller itched to remove him. But he collected himself. It wasn't as if he and Roxy were engaged. He'd made the divorce mistake once, and that was enough.

Kissing wasn't any kind of promise that he couldn't keep, he told himself, knowing he just might be full of it.

"I went out t'day." The man raised his head from Roxy's shoulder, "In my new suit from Damien's money. It got me a job."

Waller's reporter alarm went on alert. *Every bad guy has a story,* he'd told Gemma earlier. *Something good in his life that he usually buries.*

So, what the hell was going on here?

"Congratulations," Roxy said, clearly happy for him. Nonetheless, she walked the man away from the entrance, whispering to him.

Time for some lipreading.

"You remember what was said, yes?" When they were far enough away, Roxy grasped him with her hands on his padded shoulders. "No thanks are needed. That's important."

"My family owes him, Rox." He wasn't bothering to whisper. "Please tell 'im that."

"Shhh. I will, Luc, I will. Now, it's home with you. Celebrate with your wife." She kissed him on the forehead.

At this point, Waller faced away for two reasons. One, he didn't want to be seen eavesdropping, even though any other person wouldn't have understood the whispered conversation at this distance. Two, he didn't like that forehead kiss all that much, and he didn't want Roxy to see the spark of jealousy that had lit over him.

Upon returning, she sent him a shaky smile, sniffed her daisy, then took his hand to pull him into Cuffs. From the corner of his eye, Waller saw Luc wobble away, then turn back around, heading into an eatery on the corner.

Roxy didn't seem to be aware of Luc's backtracking.

"You coming in?" she asked, opening the door and letting out a hint of booze and jukebox guitar.

He nodded, followed her, then claimed his regular seat. But he couldn't stay still. He was fidgeting like a child who'd eaten too much candy.

Luc, Waller's newly minted holy grail, was just down the street, begging to be interviewed. No telling how long he'd be throwing down crawfish in that restaurant.

Then again, Roxy was here, right in front of him. He should stay with her and forget about the story for the time being. Yeah, he should definitely stay.

But that would mean giving up a damned good lead.

He glanced at the woman who'd blossomed under his touch tonight as she bustled around the bar, smiling at him every once in a while. He was also painfully aware of Duncan waiting on the customers, biding her time until she could get to Theroux again.

The ticktock of his watch thumped over his skin.

Dammit, the interview. *The interview.*

Hadn't he already gone too far to deserve a woman like Roxy, anyway? Inevitably, she was going to find out that he'd befriended her because he was going after her boss. Logic dictated that whether he told her now or later, he'd still wound her with the truth of his identity.

So why not get his story, his moment of glory? Proof that he *could* be something more than the office joke?

And maybe—just maybe—Roxy could forgive him once she saw that he was doing the right thing, exposing Theroux and combating crime.

Being a hero with the might of his pen.

When a crowd of convention-goers stumbled into the doorway declaring that this was a "real joint," they robbed him of Roxy's attentions, convinced him to go *now*.

Was he making the biggest mistake of his life by sneaking behind Roxy's back? Waller was willing to take the chance, because if there was one thing he'd learned in life, it was that daisies didn't keep forever. And if you found one and it was waiting for you two buildings down, you'd damn sure better pluck it before it died.

With that justification pounding at his brain, he left Cuffs and headed down the street.

_11_

LATER THAT NIGHT, IN THE office of Club Lotus, Damien watched on a security camera as another CEO was fleeced.

The man, Jon Straub, was an especially poetic target. Using Cayman accounts, he'd holed away money for years, duping not only his employees, but his family, as well. At least most of Theroux's targets made provisions for their wives and children. But not this bird.

As Straub sweated it out at the poker table, Kumbar entered the room. Damien didn't even tear his eyes away from the action.

He was trying so hard to enjoy this.

"Funny," he said, knowing Kumbar was listening even if he never gave a response. "I worked all my life for moments such as these. You might think I could rest after experiencing a year of such comeuppance."

Kumbar's silence agreed with Damien.

But after a few more minutes of watching Straub's chip piles dwindle, Damien couldn't tolerate it anymore. He turned off the monitor, stared at a blank screen. Due to the faint light, he could see Kumbar's barrel-like reflected image as the man crossed his arms over his chest.

"It was all supposed to be so fulfilling," Damien said. "Little did I know that I'd be falling so far as to ask you to set up a false sex club, with actors and their simulated welts and the like."

He'd even requested that Kumbar call Gem today, pretending to be a shadowy source to back up the Dante's Basement scenario. He knew reporters needed corroboration for their stories, and this was the first step in making sure she had it. Besides, Damien was anxious for her villainous piece to run in the papers, especially since Kumbar had alerted him that Bundy's boys—the most uppity gang in the city—had been talking more trash about Club Lotus, disrespecting Damien's authority over it.

He turned around to face his trusted employee. "How I expected good to come out of bad, I don't know, Kumbar. Next year, maybe it'll even get worse, though I don't know how."

The right-hand man finally spoke. "You've just got a Robin Hood complex. Steal from the rich, give to the poor. Didn't you ever read literature in school? Even Robin had trouble. The Sheriff of Nottingham was always on his ass. But you wanted this, Damien. Your psyche was asking for it, as punishment for watching your dad die and being so helpless about it at a young age."

Damien stared at Kumbar for a few seconds. "Your master's degree is showing."

"Yeah. That and a tin penny will get me a cup of chicory coffee here in the city."

"A career in security pays a whole lot better than social work, doesn't it?" Damien still remembered when he'd been putting together his businesses, when Club

Lotus had been just an angry dream. He'd hired Kumbar right off the bat because Jean had roomed with him at LSU. Recommendations didn't come much higher than one from a connected best friend.

At the moment, Kumbar was still monitoring Damien's situation.

"Want me to keep an eye on the bird for you?" he asked. "You know what comes next, anyway. Straub goes broke, you give his money to the families he's worked over, then you go on to the next case without any thanks or recognition."

Did Damien want to stay here for another hour? Not really. This place bottled him up, like a high-school lab experiment glassed in formaldehyde. Dead to the world.

"Tell you what," Damien said. "The gaming employees can close Straub out. Why don't you go and be with Kandi? You don't see each other as much as you should."

"Only by night, which might be for the best." Even though Kumbar sounded casual about it, he had an eager gleam in his dark eyes. "You coming back to Cuffs, too?"

The thought of escaping Club Lotus seemed to lift the lid from Damien's self-imposed jar. Still… "No real reason to go back to the bar."

Kumbar laughed. "Roxy called in your girl for some extra hours."

"My girl?"

Now his employee was silent again.

Of course, Damien thought. Kumbar knew when prattle didn't deserve a response.

"Go," he said, motioning Kumbar to the door.

And the man did, lickety-split. Damien wished he could be so obvious about rushing right out of here for a woman, too. Wished he had the courage to admit to himself that the only time he felt released—maybe even content—was when he was with Gem.

Damien sat in his chair for a minute longer.

So, she was at Cuffs tonight, huh?

The blood popped in his veins, robbing his head of common sense.

Turning away from his blank monitor, he decided he'd had enough of Club Lotus for tonight.

He was going to forget CEOs—and revenge—for once.

And he was going to like it, dammit.

WHEN GEMMA SAW THE COMPACT, muscled, African-American man and his pretty, Irish-lass-costumed escort go upstairs again, she sighed.

Not fair, she thought, balancing a full tray of drinks and whisking them over to a table of raucous construction workers.

Even if she knew that the man and the woman were engaged in "business," Gemma wanted to be the one on the second floor getting sweaty and lust-dizzy. But no chance of that. Damien wasn't even here tonight, but it wasn't for lack of her wishing he was.

For another hour, Gemma daydreamed and put her energy into making the customers happy. The construction workers gave her a huge tip because she'd done so well at transferring her pent-up sexual energy into joking with them, and accidentally flirting in the process.

Then, just as the crowd was thinning, it happened. Damien entered the door, dressed in his typical uniform of enigma black. If a stranger had been watching him, they would've possessed no doubt that he owned the place, because that's how he moved—with easy purpose, an authority over his surroundings.

As he leaned an arm on the bar while talking with Roxy, Gemma tried to pretend she wasn't fully aroused by something as simple as his presence. Tried to function as if her body wasn't screaming, *Here! Look over here!*

Instead, she made wiping down the tables an art, paying such attention to the details of cleaning that she almost blocked him out of her mind.

Almost.

Then she felt him next to her—the heat, the crackling awareness.

She glanced up, couldn't stop a smile. "Finally."

Even though he seemed as cool as ever, there was a definite edge to him—something she couldn't put her finger on.

"You busy?" he asked.

"Very." Gemma polished a cigar-scarred table to a…well, not a shine, but absolutely an improvement over before. "I work hard for my money."

Donna Summer's disco homage to a prostitute. How fitting. Gemma hadn't been able to help herself with that self-aimed dig.

Because even if her body was the innocent victim in all this, her brain was the culprit. It was too willing to trade lust for a story.

Teasingly, Damien wrested the towel away from her. Wasn't *he* in a feisty mood.

"Come on, Gem," he said. "We've got someplace to be."

Victory! Her body became a fairgrounds on the Fourth of July, expectancy whistling under her skin, then exploding in a shower of goose bumps.

As she followed Damien out the door, she tossed the cloth on the bar, then said goodbye to Roxy and Wedge. The older waitress wore an odd expression. Doubt?

Before going out the door, Gemma glanced around for Smith, just to wish him good-night, but she hadn't seen him since earlier. It wasn't like him to leave the altar of Roxy. Usually he saw her home.

Sweet, those two.

Then, when Damien tucked Gemma into the Galaxie, she waited for his next trick—another blindfold, a query about her next fantasy.

Where was he taking her? And did she really care as long as there was heavy breathing involved?

Without a word, he got into the car and drove them away from Cuffs, tuning the radio to a jazz station.

Still anticipating his agenda, she faced him, ready.

He caught her expectant posture. "You like jazz?"

She wasn't sure how to answer such an everyday question.

"To tell you the truth," she said, trying to predict what his seductive punch line would be, "I don't know much about it. But my tastes are eclectic, so I'll learn."

"What do you like, then?"

Hmm. A variation on their fantasy quiz game.

Surely this was leading up to something, she thought, as they traveled down Burgundy to the beautiful historic homes on Esplanade Avenue.

Gemma sighed. "I think my musical tastes are stuck in the eighties. I still wish the Police would get back together, and I adore Culture Club."

"Ah."

Either he agreed, or he wasn't going to comment on her taste.

"What about you?" she asked. "Are you a jazz aficionado?"

"I was raised on it."

She imagined a little boy with tousled black hair and pale eyes sitting on a carpet and looking up at a radio while it played Sunday-night jams. Had his life been dialed to crime at that point? Or had circumstance turned his head to vice?

Either way, she wanted to know all about him—and it wasn't only because of the story.

"Raised on it, huh?" Gemma rested her head back on the car seat, content to watch the night wind from the open window ruffle that dark hair. "And where exactly would that have been? Somewhere in the city, right?"

She already knew this, but maybe he'd go deeper during this oddly personal groove they were now in.

"I grew up in the Faubourg Marigny," he said, aiming the car onto Frenchmen Street, which would lead them above the Quarter and into the area itself.

As if to interrupt the flow of conversation, he turned up the radio, pointed to it. "Here's a song."

A saxophone buttered some notes over the whisper

of drums and a bass. Gemma wasn't sure whether he really liked the melody or had just wanted to shut her up.

But she didn't have long to wonder because, within minutes, they'd pulled along a curb. As he cut the engine and got out of the car, live jazz took the place of the radio.

He helped her out, and she detected where the music was coming from. A yellow cottage with ivy creeping over the walls and men hanging out by the porch while smoking cigars.

What does Damien have up his sleeve? she thought. More peignoirs? More what-can-we-get-away-with sex?

Her pulse kicked, ratcheted up a notch. Whatever it was, she was willing.

He planted his palm in the small of her back and led her inside, exchanging hellos with the guys at the entrance. Then, once through the door, a cloud of acrid smoke greeted them, the ceiling fans only serving to fuse the stench of cigarettes and the mugginess together.

But, as in every other place in the city, no one seemed to notice the risk to their health, thought Gemma, who'd been raised to be a vigilant SoCal nonsmoker.

Nope. Everyone was laughing, cigarettes drooping from between their fingers while holding ice-choked drinks in their other hands. The beat of a tune from the onstage band drowned out the merriment with its melancholy notes.

This wasn't a tourist trap. Gemma knew that much. She could tell from the drinks a place served. Bourbon

Street bars peddled poisons, like Hand Grenades and Horny Gators, in collectible glasses. Joints like this one, with no screaming neon to announce its name, were the real deal.

Once again, Gemma asked herself what the catch was. What kind of games were being played behind closed doors, and when would Damien ask her to participate?

As he guided Gemma to a table near the stage and dance floor, Damien nodded to several groups who toasted him with their drinks, sending up a welcoming cheer. And when the two of them were seated, a shorts-clad waitress took their order. He wanted beer and gumbo. She wanted a diet cola.

"Is that all?" he asked in her ear, overcoming the loud music as the waitress left them.

"For now," she yelled back, letting a saucy smile do the double-talking for her. She wanted a whole lot of things from him. Things you couldn't order from a wait-ress.

The band was evidently at the tail end of a set, so Damien and Gemma reclined in their cheap vinyl seats, listening to the three-piece ensemble backing up The Incredible Big Iggy, as a placard above the stage read. The group included a lead guitarist wearing a black beret, a female drummer with Laverne DeFazio glasses and butch black hair and a bassist nestled in the corner with his slick goatee.

The front man, Iggy, weighed so much that Gemma feared for his health. Sitting on a stool, with a half beard, tinted glasses and a blue polo shirt, he had to clock in at nearly four hundred pounds. But his voice was as smooth as the moon's tide, laving over each song with a range so amazing that even Gemma—the jazz virgin—fell a little in love with him.

When the band took a break, she found Damien's gaze on her.

"What?" she said in the sudden silence, grabbing on to her soda for something to occupy her. "I like it. Didn't you expect me to?"

"I thought maybe the Beach Boys would be more your style." She could tell by his grin that he was joshing her.

"Hey, let's not rule surf music out." She rested an elbow on the table. "Do you hang out here often? Everyone seems to be your pal."

He leaned forward in his chair, too, stirred his gumbo until steam rose out of it. "I started coming to see Big Ig when I was a kid, sneaking out at dusk to meet my friend here. Jean and I used to listen by the door and talk the neighbors into rolling some dice with us. We took lots of money, Jean and I."

A faint smile lit over his face, then disappeared.

Jean Dulac, an up-and-coming crime boss. His good friend.

"You seem sad right now," Gemma said, testing the moment.

"It's nothing."

Right. It was something about Jean, something that had shaded the pale of Damien's eyes until he'd chased it away.

In a masterful move of avoidance, he scooped

gumbo into his spoon, blew on it. Then he held it out to her.

"It's too late to be eating." She never chowed down past eight o'clock, no matter what her schedule was like. The structure of her habits had always maintained her weight. That, and a long jog every other day.

Obviously, her rigid rules didn't matter to him. He nudged her pursed lips with the spoon, grinning. Warm, wet spices tickled her lips.

"You're in New Orleans," he said. "Live a little."

The smell of it was delicious. A bite wouldn't hurt. Besides, she was already doing some major living since meeting Theroux. Why stop now?

She opened her mouth, and he slid the spoon inside, his eyes darkening as she sucked in the thick gumbo. Heaven.

Her eyelids fluttered shut, then opened again as she savored it.

"The best stuff around," he said. He'd donned that hooded gaze, that sleepy look of intensity he wore when aroused.

Gemma held her breath, waiting for the next step. The dirty talk, the proposition.

But he just dug into the gumbo, devouring it, offering her more.

Miffed, Gemma shook her head. "I'm full."

"A teaspoon will do that to a girl so slight as you," he said, grinning again. "Not that I'm saying you're too skinny, Gem. I mean that you're just right."

He hadn't said it in a seductive manner. Just very matter-of-factly. Gemma didn't know why, but his unadorned honesty overwhelmed her, made her concentrate on stirring the ice around in her soda.

"Thanks," she murmured, happy to be complimented.

Soon, the band came back on stage to a wealth of applause.

Iggy spoke into his microphone. "Now's about time for some dance music. Get yourselves on the floor."

And, with that, they ripped into "Mustang Sally," Iggy's voice taming the lyrics with raw passion.

Damien tapped his fingers on the table. Looked at Gemma. Tapped them some more.

She held back her amusement, realizing he might be nervous about asking her to dance.

Damien Theroux, a shy boy?

When she caught his gaze, she let him off the hook, nodding toward the filling dance floor. Relief seemed to embrace him as he stood, took her hand in his.

The music's beat was sassy, but as fluid as a Sunday walk through the Quarter. The tempo offered a choice: "fast dancing," as a junior-high student would say, where the participants didn't touch, or "slow dancing."

Damien chose the slow route, resting his hands on her hips while she took hold of his shoulders. Barely moving except for the lazy sway of their bodies, they locked gazes.

But they were always doing that, Damien thought. Watching. Reading. Waiting for information to erupt in an unguarded moment.

He didn't want to think about agendas now, because for once in his life, he didn't feel hammered down, pinned under the weight of responsibility. He felt like a normal fellow, out for a good time on a weeknight with his girl, dancing to old tunes.

Even though a tight longing was stretching him to the limit, he relished the sensual pain of it. Was Gem feeling the same way? Was she disappointed because he wasn't leading her through one of those fantasies?

Was he enough for her without them?

As "Mustang Sally" came to a halt, Iggy eased into some very sultry Otis Redding. Without hesitation, Gem moved her arms around Damien's neck and cuddled her head against his shoulder. She exhaled against his shirt, over his heart, encasing it with warmth.

Tentatively, he smoothed his hands on her back, rubbing the slope of it. When he'd been a kid loitering outside the doors of this place, he used to imagine the adults inside, used to wonder if he'd ever be lucky enough to bring a woman here.

Look at him now. Damien had never, ever invited anyone with him to see Iggy. There hadn't been time, he'd always told himself. There'd never been a purpose.

Cautiously, he rested his chin on Gem's head. She had no idea that he'd opened up, even in this small way. But that was for the best. The knowledge of it would give her a power he couldn't lose.

He would just enjoy this secret moment himself.

As usual.

For the next hour, the band played songs from Wilson Pickett to Marvin Gaye, and Damien managed to stay on the floor for all of it. If Jean or Kumbar saw him now, he'd be a laughingstock. But he didn't mind so much. Gem was arching her neck, laughing, enjoying herself so much that he couldn't help wanting to please her more and more.

Finally, it was time for another break, and they returned to the table. He ordered another beer and soda while pushing in Gem's chair for her.

"This is something," she said, cheeks flushed, blue eyes sparkling. "I wish I could've grown up around here."

"No, you don't." The words were out before he could stop them.

Gem seemed genuinely interested. "Why?"

Aw, hell. Maybe he could go with this conversation, keep that glow on her without doing much damage. "There's a lot of opportunity for trouble. It's not easy for a kid to turn it down."

She tucked a pin back in her hair. The blond upsweep had started coming down while they danced, but Damien wished she would just leave it.

He reached out, stilled her hand, getting his message across. Biting her lip, Gem received the signal loud and clear, winging a stray hair behind her ear instead.

"So you were a juvenile delinquent?" she asked.

His first instinct was to lie, to pile on the BS for her reporter's edification. But he didn't. "I got in a few scrapes with Jean's help, but I knew anything worse would light my *papa*'s temper. He wouldn't tolerate mischief, much like my *maman*."

"Oh, one of those tough childhoods, then."

She had a sympathetic tilt to her brow, one that Damien didn't think was fake or goading.

"Not tough at all." Not until his *papa*'s death, at least. "My parents were the most a boy could ask for. They wanted me to grow up right."

Gem hesitated. "What did they do when you started your...businesses?"

"*Papa* was already dead."

The words were flat, rushed. He didn't want her to know how profoundly his father's passing had affected him. It would've been like reopening a wound so she could pour salt into it.

Still, she seemed to look past his body language. She rested her hand on his knee below the table, but it wasn't a come-on. The gesture was comforting, like a blanket covering his sick body on a cold day.

"And your mom?" she asked.

A tug-of-war was raging within him. Answer or stay silent? Would she dig up the information, anyway? Had she already done so?

What the hell. "She's gone, too. A couple years back." He shook his head, smiled. "Stubborn till her last day, that woman. Even when I got some money in my pockets, she wouldn't move from the old cottage. Stayed in the same damned place, even though I bought her a new one in the Quarter."

Gem was smiling, as if she'd known his *maman,* too. It drew a connecting electric wire between them, that smile. Attached her heart to his in a way.

"Did your life bother her?" she asked. "Is that why she wouldn't accept your money?"

Perceptive little reporter.

When he didn't answer, she did the talking. "I can't

help noticing right now, Damien, that the underworld seems to be bothering you, too."

Was his expression that opaque? Immediately, he shifted in his chair so that Gem's hand fell away from his knee. The patch of skin where she'd been touching him burned in the aftermath, cooling quickly.

"I've got no qualms," he said, steel in his comment.

Their conversation lapsed as they both drank. After a few minutes, he couldn't stand it anymore. He helped her out of her chair and took her back to the car.

She didn't protest, probably realizing that she'd shut him down for the night, anyway.

As he drove to her Garden District corner—silly, really, because in spite of the fake address she'd provided for Roxy, he'd discovered that she lived in a converted apartment nearby—Damien felt desperate. He'd lost his sense of self back at Iggy's, lost the initiative over her.

As he completed the pantomime of dropping her off, she leaned in the window, probably to say thank-you.

He beat her to the punch. "One thing, Gem."

Her eyebrows rose along with the tips of her mouth. "Yes?"

Summoning all the strength, the bitterness he had left in him, Damien dealt his last card, saving himself. "Tell me your next fantasy."

He could see the disappointment envelop her. But then, fast as a flicker, the reporter returned full force as she traded emotion for ambition.

She tilted her head, flashed some cleavage at him.

"This is strange, but I've always wondered what it'd

feel like to be someone else during sex," she said, voice husky. "Even the opposite gender. Isn't that crazy?"

Was she making fantasies up at this point? Not even Gem seemed to be invested in this one. But maybe that was because he'd gone from hot to cold so quickly with her.

Damn his loss of composure. "Then I'll see you tomorrow."

And he left her, never looking back. His parting was exactly as it should have been—business as usual.

For both of them.

He didn't sleep well that night. The lacy undies Gem had allowed him to slide off of her were still in his bedside drawer, and even the feel of them didn't yank him out of his Romeo yearning for her.

It was only when Kumbar woke him up before the sun rose that Damien truly got his fire back.

"Bundy's boys," he said while they talked in Damien's parlor. "They used guns to intercept the club's money as it was being shuttled to the souvenir shop."

Where the cash was laundered.

Under his robe, Damien's flesh bristled. "Are you telling me I was robbed?"

"I wish I wasn't." Kumbar tossed a daily newspaper onto a table. "And this has got to be the reason."

Through a red haze, Damien read the headline. "Theroux the Philanthropist," it screamed.

By Waller Smith.

Barely containing his rage, Damien picked up the paper, scanned the article. Everything was in there: How he used Club Lotus's winnings to bail out poor families. All his weaknesses. All good excuses for Bundy to sic his dogs on him—the weak member of the pack—and think he'd get away with it.

Someone at the *Advocate-Tribune* must have tipped off Bundy so he could move last night, before Damien expected it.

That's why payoffs were worth the investment. Too bad Damien hadn't thought of it first.

Kumbar said his next piece with trepidation. "I don't know if Gem helped Waller Smith with this, but I'll check into it."

Damien was beyond anger. Now he was ice—cold, methodical. A fool no longer.

"Do that, Kumbar. And while you're at it, I'll be doing my own homework."

It was time for another trip to Dante's Basement for Gem. But, this time, it would have little to do with her fantasies.

And a lot to do with payback.

12

THAT MORNING, WALLER SAT in front of Nancy Mendoza's desk in the *Weekly Gossip*'s offices, an unlit celebration cigar clamped between his teeth as she thrust the *Advocate-Tribune,* a competing newspaper, at him. His headline blared like an Olympic fanfare.

"You went behind my back?" she asked, her rosy-tanned skin flaring with temper.

Waller took out the cigar, spread out his arms in a wide shrug. "They're a daily, chief. The *Gossip* doesn't come out until Sunday. As a fellow journalist, I'm sure you understand that this was too big to sit on. And I told you, I'm here to quit, anyway. The *AT* made me an offer I couldn't refuse."

One that would buy all the daisies in the world for Roxy. After all, how could she hate a story like this? She *had* to be proud of her boss, seeing as he wasn't actually a true criminal. Theroux had saved a lot of families from ruin by sticking it to crooked rich men.

Still, something was bugging Waller: why had Roxy been so vehement with Luc about keeping silent?

As he chomped on his cigar, he knew there was an even deeper story he hadn't unearthed last night.

Waller had been so busy interviewing Luc, pitching the article to a friend at the *Advocate-Tribune* and then doing all the footwork, that he hadn't been able to talk with Roxy. Though he would have liked to hear her side of events, there just hadn't been time. He'd been busy tracking Luc's backup sources, tightening up the basic Robin Hood angle.

Nancy threw the paper at him, causing Waller to duck.

"Gemma Duncan was working on this for us. You scooped a co-worker. Did you realize that?"

So Duncan had never told Nancy about his headline race with her. Was it because of the young reporter's pride? Because she didn't want to seem like the playground tattletale?

Or was it because she'd been so damned sure that her A+-student self would beat him?

Now pride flooded *him*. He'd come out the winner—do-nothing, layabout Waller Smith.

"Duncan can write a longer piece for you in the *Weekly,* so don't go throwing papers at me." Waller rubbed his eyes. This time he was sleepy because he'd gotten only two hours of slumber at the most. But *this* exhaustion was well earned, cleansing.

He'd finally written a positive story for the better of mankind. Not a bad night's work.

Nancy was still raging, shooting Waller the Look of Instant Death. "So there you both were, hanging around Cuffs. I just hope you didn't blow Gemma's cover. You're out of the game, but she's still working on this story."

Waller gestured to his headline, unable to hold back

a huge smile. "Theroux's not as bad as he wants everyone to believe."

"You'd better be sure. He called Gemma this morning, and she went with him somewhere."

Waller froze in his seat, remembering the alley, the cheater. The punches.

But why was he worried? Theroux didn't know that Duncan was a journalist. He wasn't even aware that she and Waller knew each other outside of the bar.

Still, his reporter sense flashed neon red.

Theroux had taken Duncan *somewhere*. The morning that Waller's article had come out.

Even though Waller had discovered Theroux's softer side, he also knew that the man was well-versed in revenge—he merely used the results of it for good.

If Theroux knew Duncan had been out to uncover him…

Waller threw down his cigar and burst out of his seat. "I'll clean out my desk later, chief. I'm going to track Duncan down."

"Why? What—"

"We'll talk later. Just—" he gestured madly toward the phone "—try to get her on the cell."

"I'll try."

They had to do better than try. With all the stars in his eyes, he'd forgotten—conveniently?—that his story would put *her* in jeopardy. "I'm gonna track her down, Nancy."

With that, Waller whipped out his own phone, then sped out of the office and toward the elevator bank. Who could tell him where Duncan had gone with Theroux? Sure, maybe he was jumping out of his skin for nothing, but...

He punched the down button, then paced back and forth, doing a double take as he caught a glimpse of red hair near his desk.

Red hair. Mae West hips. Pale skin.

Roxy.

Waller's blood expanded, making him catch his breath. Automatically, he smiled. Had she been waiting for him to get to work?

That's when she met his gaze. Judging by the look on her face, this wasn't a congratulatory call. Her expression didn't change as she ambled over to him, no smiles, just a confused puddle of questions glistening in her eyes.

Without a word, Roxy held out the paper, the headline facing up.

The words screamed at him, the noise only adding to his urgency with Duncan and Theroux.

"I know," Waller said, seizing Roxy's hand and guiding her into the elevator. Once there, he assaulted the button board, repeatedly pushing the garage-floor command. "We have a lot to talk about, but I need your help right now."

"Do you?" She rolled up the newspaper, tucked it under her arm. Her lack of temper stung worse than a dressing-down. "I think maybe I gave you enough help."

"Roxy...?"

"Damien knew, Waller. I also knew you and Gem were reporters, from the get-go. I agreed to lead you to a story. We just didn't expect you to find the wrong one."

Waller almost fell backward from her confession. She'd been working him as much as the other way around? Not that this made him feel better. "Listen, there're a lot of reasons I walked into Cuffs that first night, but they changed with every passing second I got to know you."

The elevator light dinged for the third floor, and Waller's heartbeat spiked.

"Roxy, hop in my car with me. Hear me out, would you? And, most important of all, please tell me where Theroux and Duncan...um...Gem...no, Gemma, are right now. I'm worried about her. No matter what you or Theroux might think, she had nothing to do with what I published."

With a sidelong look, Roxy conveyed her own concern. "He took her somewhere? This *morning?*"

"That's what I hear."

Roxy exhaled as the elevator stopped. When the doors flew open, both of them rushed into the parking garage.

Her voice echoed off the concrete. "He was upset when I talked to him on the phone two hours ago, but he won't take it out on Gem."

"You don't sound too sure about that."

Roxy paused. "All right. I've never heard him this full of rage. Certainly, with those CEOs, he was livid, but now... Waller, a rival hit Club Lotus last night. I'm sure it was because your article convinced them that Damien was an easy target. People in his position don't give away their earnings. You made him sound soft, and I can guarantee Bundy Sonnier took a lot of pleasure in taking Damien down a peg or two. One less competitor means more business for his own gaming room." Roxy shook her head. "That's what he feared, you know. That once his competitors found out the truth, they would pounce on him. And he was right."

They got to Waller's compact car, the gray body looking as if it'd been slapped around by the streets.

"I didn't see it that way," Waller said. "Damien's a great local hero. He's changed a lot of lives, Roxy. Even if he was running an illegal establishment, he was doing it for the right reasons."

"But he can't do it no more. You've seen to that. He can't keep that club now. There'll be no customers because they think they'll be fleeced. Besides he's a laughingstock to his competition."

Just as Waller used to be. Was his journalistic elevation worth the price of Theroux's destruction?

Waller's shoulders slumped as he started the car. The body was ugly, but the engine ran like gold. "I'm sorry, but…" There was no time to go into his reasons for exposing Theroux right now. "Where do you think he took Gemma?"

Roxy motioned toward the cell phone still in his hand. "Kumbar's going to know, if the man will talk."

He handed the device to her and she dialed, giving them some direction, some peace of mind.

And as Waller pulled out of the parking garage while Roxy did her own investigative work, he knew he still had a lot of explaining to do to a woman whose opinion mattered more than anything.

WHEN "GEM"'S PHONE HAD trilled Gemma awake this morning, she'd thought, in her sleep-worn haze, that Damien was calling to smooth things over between them.

She should have known better.

"Time for a fantasy," he'd said.

She'd had just enough time to shower, call Nancy to tell her what was going on and grab a protein bar for breakfast. And, when she'd tumbled out the front door of her house-turned-apartment complex, forgetting everything from her keys to Gem's phone in her haste, Damien had surprised her by waiting at the curb in his car.

At her curious gaze, he hadn't shown any emotion.

"I've always known," he'd said, nodding to the slim house with lacy curtains and a wrought-iron fence.

She'd gulped. Her Cuffs paperwork had reflected a fake Garden District address. So how…?

From that point on, the ride had been silent.

Now, as Damien pulled up to a building on Dauphine, Gemma's intuition was throwing a fit.

Something was off.

She got out of the car without waiting for him to help, clutched her purse, which contained pepper spray. The sky rumbled with the threat of a thunderstorm. On either side, they were surrounded by colorfully splashed buildings, including an abandoned four-story baby-blue with curtainless windows, and the Dauphine Inn.

She knew this hotel.

Especially the second-story windows, because she'd gotten a good view of them the other night.

Slowly, her gaze traveled to the deserted building on the other side of the street.

Dante's Basement.

Damien strolled to the door, then held it open, a shadow against the light of day. He wanted to complete another fantasy. Was it the one she'd created on the spot last night? The mumbo jumbo about being another person during sex?

Her conscience had been working overtime then, hadn't it? Guilt speaking through her small talk.

Sucking up all her courage, Gemma walked past him.

Surveying the dusty furniture and chandelier that greeted her, she thought, *Faded glory.* This time, there was no French music to serenade her. No whips snapping in naughty invitation.

"I've got something for you in our room," he said, holding his hand toward the stairs.

"I'm sure you do." Was her voice shaking? Dammit, it'd better not be.

She headed up, knowing exactly which room he was talking about. When she got there, muted light drizzled through the window, reflecting a dull sky. The sex toys were gone. The washbowl was dry, except for the reminder of petal fragments clinging to the porcelain. The armoire was empty, except for one costume and a newspaper folded on the wood beneath it.

The memory of their passion lingered, as fragile as a spiderweb. As she walked to the armoire, she tingled with flashes of their night together: The slick condensation on the window glass against her breasts. The feel of him slipping into her. The coolness of sheets against their skin after they had retired to the bed for more.

She inspected the armoire's costume. Odd. Gray pants connected to black suspenders. A sleeveless T-shirt. A blue-and-white-striped tie. A matching fedora. A gray jacket with a laminated card clipped to the lapel.

PRESS, it said.

Gemma's throat went dry, scratchy with nerves.

"Put it on," Damien said as he came next to her, tone measured, so unlike the last time he'd made the request.

She just stared at the clothing.

Damien took out the fedora. "You wanted to be someone else. How about Clark Kent without the glasses?"

He knew.

"I—"

Gently fisting a handful of her still-damp hair, which she'd left down today in her haste to get ready, he scooped the fedora over it. Then he tucked the stray strands inside, pausing to inspect his work. Briefly, a splinter of something like remorse invaded his gaze, but then he sauntered away, giving her the feeling that he expected her to finish dressing.

"I apologize for last night," he said when he was finally across the room, by the bed. The springs creaked as he sat down. "Our time together didn't end well. I wanted to get back into your…well, good graces, so here we have another fantasy. Partly yours, partly mine."

"Damien, I know—"

He held up a hand. "Humor me, *chérie,* I've had a rough morning." The planes of his face hardened for an instant. Then, as if he knew better, he erased his emotions.

"Here's the game—you can ask any question of me you desire, but there's a cost. For every one, you must take off a piece of clothing. You can be another person for a time, but in the end, I want to be inside of *you*. So you see," he said, leveling a nerve-shattering smile at her, "we both benefit from this."

She was quaking. From fear? Anticipation? She wasn't sure what. But she wanted to stay, not run. Wanted *him* to strip down, too. Wanted him to reveal the man he'd shown her last night.

The man she'd felt comfortable with, a bad boy with good underneath the skin. She didn't even care that, with such a guy, her story would evaporate.

With a start, she realized she could love a man like last night's Damien, one who saw into the soul of jazz, who made her feel like the most desirable woman in creation and who didn't seem to buy his own publicity at times.

Was the potential worth fighting for?

She dropped her purse and the pepper spray with it. "Close your eyes," she said softly.

He did, and she shed her shorts and tank top for the reporter's costume, ready for battle.

"Open up," she said, meaning it.

When he looked her up and down, his gaze had a regretful cruelty to it.

Thunder shook the window as the storm geared up. Fully dressed, she walked toward him, an old-time reporter, hands tucked in pockets and fedora dipped over her eyes.

THE ENEMY, DAMIEN THOUGHT. Gem was one of *them*, a journalist who had cut him open and allowed Club Lotus to bleed dead. There would be no more customers, no more CEOs willing to gamble with Theroux.

Besides, the stakes were too high now. Already, Jean was threatening to exact revenge on Bundy and his boys, and Damien didn't want his friend to start an underground war for this.

No, Damien's taste for revenge was focused elsewhere now. Bundy had only taken advantage of the situation—Waller Smith and Gemma Duncan had created it.

If only he could take more pleasure in seeing this punishment through. Punishment for pointing out his weaknesses and failures.

He slapped the thought aside. "First question."

Rain started to tap on the glass. This was it—the fulfillment of her ambition, an interview with Damien Theroux. She'd better enjoy it while it lasted.

But she was hesitating. Why? Wasn't this her big chance?

"You don't want to know why I'm such a menace to society?" he asked.

She took a step closer. "How long have you known?"

"A while. Take off the hat."

"That answer's not—"

"These are the rules, Gem." He stood from the mattress. "Question, answer, strip."

In a show of spirit, she whipped off the hat, her blond hair tumbling past her shoulders. Hunger twisted in

Damien's groin, but there was something in his chest, too. Hesitant warmth.

He tamped it down. "Good. Next."

"Why didn't you let me know that you knew?"

Casually, he moved to the armoire, as if this whole process wasn't affecting him. He removed the newspaper, tapped it against his thigh as he drew next to her.

"It didn't suit my purposes to let you know. Now the jacket comes off for that one."

An exasperated huff. The removal of the big gray jacket. The rain knocking on the window.

Hammering against his better instincts.

He slid the paper, headline up, into her hands. As she read, her eyes widened. When she finished, she dropped it to the floor like so much trash.

Hope lit within him. She didn't know about this?

Then again, Gem had been acting ever since they'd met. He had no reason to buy into her deception again.

"Damien?" she asked. Her eyes were moist, as if his charitable deeds touched her.

"Is that a question?"

"Yes."

Pissed—at Waller, at her, at the whole damned world—Damien tugged off one side of her suspenders, revealing the outline of a breast through the thin T-shirt. She hadn't worn a bra, the pro.

She left the elastic fabric hanging there, a tear trickling down her face, echoing the rain.

He prowled to her other side. "Yes, the story is true, and thanks to Luc Brulatour, everyone knows it."

Luc. Damien couldn't be angry with the man, especially after all the hard knocks he'd survived. But he had to take this out on someone. That's how life worked.

"Next question?" he said.

"No." She turned while he circled. "The article tells about the fleecing and the charity, but I want to know why. None of the interviews revealed that."

Though a part of Damien couldn't help wanting her to relieve his burden, he wouldn't answer. He'd lived so long with the agony of his *papa*'s shame and death that it had become like a second heart—one that was shielded by the much colder organ he'd created to cover his real anguish.

This time, instead of forcing her other suspender down, he eased it, slowly, exposing the hint of pink nipple under her shirt. Both tips hardened under his unwavering gaze.

"It's simple, Gem," he said. "Nowadays, I've got so much money I don't know what to do with it. Robbing big businessmen then redistributing the wealth keeps me honest."

"You're lying."

"Next."

Her forehead wrinkled, introducing an expression of pure frustration. Why did that look have the power to destroy him?

"So the prostitution. Dante's Basement." She shook her head. "They never existed?"

"Just for you." Taking his time, he stood in front of her, undid her tie—which hadn't been done properly in the first place—then allowed it to slither down between them to the floor.

"Why did you do it all, Damien? Your answers are too vague."

"That clearly infuriates you. We're not playing this game for the sake of getting something published."

"I know why we're playing it."

He undid her pants, the zipper. The metal moaned as he downed it, fingers brushing between her legs at the same time.

She smacked his hand away. "Why did you invent Dante's?"

"Because I wanted you to spread the gospel. A little scary news goes a long way, Gem. Unfortunately, this bit of positive news in the paper has already done its damage."

"What do you mean?"

"First, the last question." He slipped her pants down her legs, and she kicked them away. "Now…" He whipped off her T-shirt, leaving her naked except for a pair of innocent white lace panties. So this was what she wore when she wasn't in Cuffs uniform.

The purity almost undid Damien.

As he told her about the Club Lotus robbery, he allowed himself to cup one palm under her jaw—that square jaw, so out of place on such a sweet face.

"Your story closed down my club," he finished, grip tightening. He let go of her, afraid to bruise or wound, wishing he was the type of man who didn't mind strong-arming to get his way.

The life he'd chosen would have been so much easier that way.

"*My* story?" She covered her chest with her arms, a

conflicted smile of irony seeming to rip her apart from the inside out. "Damn Waller."

"Why? Because you didn't write it?"

When she paused, Damien lost his grip on the slow hope he'd been kindling.

"Funny," she said. "A couple weeks ago, all I wanted was to find a huge headline. I heard you and Lamont talking, and I thought, this is it—my big break. Everything was going my way until my co-worker, Waller, decided this was his kind of muckraking, too. But so what? I was going to be a real reporter, not some tabloid hack who has to defend her existence to her family and everyone who asks what she does for a living. But..."

"But now?"

She met his gaze, and he had to turn away from the honesty of her visual contact.

"Now I see that stories don't end after you write them. Damien, I thought you were a criminal. You wanted me to believe it, too. Logically, I'd be doing the world a favor by warning them about how you worked. But who am I kidding?" She offered a now-I-know-better laugh. "I was overreaching, anyway. I was born to write about pregnant geriatric strippers and their cupcake lovers. So bring on the urban legends. I'm back in business."

Damien realized he wasn't talking to Gem James anymore. This was a woman he didn't know, with goals and heartfelt dreams he had no idea about.

Or did he? How much of herself had she revealed during this charade?

He started to move away from her. He didn't care

about Gem, or Gemma, or whoever she was. She'd set out to ruin his life, bringing Waller with her as a consequence. He had no need for a woman like this.

Even if every cell in his body told him he did.

Gemma stepped in front of him, removing her arms from her breasts to hold a hand against his heart, the simple gesture startling him.

"Next question," she said, voice thick with emotion. "Why won't you admit that, deep down, you're not so bad?"

He'd been playing a game of deception with himself for so long that he couldn't bring himself to admit he had any decency. Decency had lost him Club Lotus—the only way he could keep his *papa* alive, vindicated.

"Because." He grabbed her wrist, preparing to remove her hand from him. To remove the chills of lust—and something way more dangerous—that her touch inspired. "Hate drives me. That's what I'm made of."

"You're desperate to stay bad, aren't you?" Gemma grabbed his shirt with her other hand, clearly unwilling to let go of him. "It keeps people away, just like you hoped the 'crime lord' story would do. Isn't that right?"

He didn't answer. Too stunned. Afraid of the truth.

"Bad men don't get close," she said, moving toward him. "Bad men don't get intimate."

She was pulling him to her, pressing against him, her breasts so soft against his chest. Damien melted, closing his eyes, unable to fight his body's demands.

He felt the brush of warm air over his mouth, realized her lips were poised next to his.

"Kiss me," she said with the same sense of command he used when ordering her to don a costume.

Panic shot through him, mixing with boiled blood and scattered emotions. He bent a little lower.

Felt her suck in a breath.

A kiss. Simple, pure, washing everything from black to white. Already, he felt the color bleed out of him, leaving him weaker than ever.

Vulnerable to another attack.

He pulled away, leaving Gemma standing there, bared and unguarded. This time, she didn't cover herself.

But she didn't have to. Her wounds couldn't be hidden—they were in the blue pools of her eyes, open for him to see and regret.

"You'll never be able to let go," she said. "Hatred, darkness—whatever it is that you've fallen in love with."

Love. The word rocked him.

While he took support against a bed pole, she walked to the pile of discarded clothing and started to put herself back together. She chose to wear the reporter's garb, and the significance wasn't lost on Damien.

Her other life was more important than he was.

Silence reigned, but it was only because he was trying to search for the right things to say. The things that would keep her here long enough for him to explain why he was having such a hard time letting go.

But as the words escaped his second, hidden, heart, rushing toward the tip of his tongue, the downstairs door crashed open. Voices called, "Gemma?" and one of them sounded like Roxy's. Footsteps banged up the stairs.

As Damien glanced at Gemma, an unreadable expression covered her face—relief? Was she happy to be saved from all that hatred he couldn't betray?

It was the ultimate rejection. A perfect reason for him to stay true to himself.

Seconds later, Waller Smith, the reporter who'd brought him down, stood in the doorway, and Roxy hovered right in back of him, shaking her head at Damien's folly.

13

"DUNCAN," WALLER SAID, PANTING by the door, "you're safe."

Gemma couldn't believe this. An inner maelstrom blinded her, preventing her from settling into one emotion.

Inferiority, because Waller had beat her to the story she'd coveted to the point of distraction.

Shame, because she was wearing the reporter's outfit—caught in one of her idiotic fantasies.

Sadness, because Damien Theroux had rejected her after she'd offered her heart to him.

Shock, because *he*—not her desire to win awards or job advancement—was all that really mattered in the end.

As Roxy peeked into the room over Waller's shoulder, Gemma's face heated up. They had to be wondering about her strange costume.

"Let's go," Waller said, holding his hand out to Gemma while casting a cautious glance toward Damien.

The reporter looked like a lion tamer pinning a wild beast into a corner with his hypnotic gaze. If Gemma hadn't felt so beaten down, she would have laughed at the image.

At the thought of Waller coming to rescue her.

"No," Damien said and, for a second, Gemma perked up, thinking he was going to tell Waller to scram. That he wanted to be alone with her and work everything out.

That he wanted to give her that long-delayed kiss.

But as he moved away from the bed and toward the door, Gemma's chest closed on itself, a cave-in of grief.

Was Damien going to smash Waller to a pulp now? Was he going to stay a tough guy and prove that she'd been right about him clinging to his hatred?

Obviously, the older reporter thought so. His green eyes flared while he braced his legs boxer-style.

Then Roxy stepped in front him, arm outstretched to halt Damien. As Waller's mouth gaped open, Theroux froze, his own face also arranged in disbelief.

"Do you think so little of me, Roxy?" he asked.

"I know you won't hurt him," she said. "But don't you leave without hearing him out."

He dragged a stormy glare toward Gemma. Even though it spoke volumes, she couldn't decipher it.

Or maybe it was an echo of her final words to him:

You'll never be able to let go. Hatred, darkness— whatever it is that you've fallen in love with.

He was never going to change, was he? The chances of him listening to their justifications were zero to none.

Or maybe his eyes were telling her more than even *that*. They reflected an endless remorse, a longing so painful that it drilled into Gemma's gut.

Before she could react, he doused the emotion, looked away, addressed Roxy.

"Like it or not, I am leaving. Step aside. I haven't the time for this."

Roxy assessed him, gave an understanding nod of compromise, then backed Waller into the hallway.

As Damien exited, he ignored the older reporter, probably because facing him would have stirred up everything he'd just buried.

Dammit, she had to give this one last try.

"Damien!" His name caught in her throat.

As a response, he raised a hand in the air and stopped in the doorway, his back to Gemma. *No more,* the gesture seemed to say. Then he turned his head ever so slightly toward Roxy.

"She can get her personal effects from Cuffs tonight," he said. "I won't be around."

Without any further ado, he left, just as if they'd never even touched each other—physically, mentally…

Emotionally.

None of them moved as his footsteps retreated down the stairs, out the door.

Out of her life.

But that's obviously what he wanted; he couldn't stand to see her again after all her lies. Even if Damien Theroux had stretched open her life like the edges of a black hole, allowing her to dive in and enjoy the new sensations, that had been the extent of his interest in her.

God, she thought, their encounters had never been about love—just lust. Mind-expanding physical explosions that had forced her to question what she really wanted, who she really was.

There'd never been anything more.

As his car roared away from the building, the possibility of never seeing him again left an empty space inside of Gemma, like a piano that was missing a key.

Finally, Roxy and Waller stepped back into the room. "You okay?" Waller repeated.

"Yeah." The answer was too soft, unsure. Trying again, Gemma blinked, straightened her spine. "Yeah, everything's fine."

When Waller started to ask a question, Roxy nudged him. Good. Gemma didn't feel like talking now.

"Need a ride?" the head waitress asked, holding herself at a distance. Gemma couldn't blame her. She'd fooled Roxy with her undercover act, also.

Gemma nodded, and the redhead started down the hallway.

"Then we'll talk in the car," her boss said. "This place gives me the willies. I don't know why Damien keeps it."

With a last glance out the curtainless window, Gemma took in the hotel across the street. The blank windows signified the thrill of being caught. Of having another person see you at your most intimate.

She understood why Damien held on to this place.

She just wished she understood more.

KNEES ALMOST TUCKED TO HER chest, Gemma sat in the back seat of Waller's beat-up compact car. She had just finished telling Roxy about everything.

All the apologies were keeping Gemma's mind off

Damien. At least, that's what she told herself. In fact, as Waller took his turn and related the details of his investigation to Roxy, Gemma sank farther into the vinyl, realizing what a failure she was.

No more Lois Lane fantasies.

Gemma Duncan was a tabloid reporter, and that's the best she would ever do. After all, this wasn't the first time she'd been scooped. When she'd been fired from her first job in Orange County, she'd promised herself it would never happen again.

And it had.

With a twinge of fresh anguish, Gemma clung to her knees. If there were a report card for careers, she'd earn an F.

Waller had stopped explaining, leaving Roxy to watch the Central Business District traffic pass by, arms crossed over her chest. He shot a panicked glance into the back seat, and Gemma helplessly shrugged, unable to give him advice on how to win Roxy back.

What did she know about romance? Her relationship skills took second place only to her ineptitude in the reporting category.

"Well, then," Roxy said to the window after an appropriate amount of tortuous silence, "if I was a hypocrite, I'd ask you to let me out of this tin can, so as to put a distance between me and the two of you skunks. But seeing as I was a skunk, too, I can't do that." She turned away from the window, unfolded her arms.

She'd already explained about *her* part in the charade—how Theroux had persuaded her to feed Waller false information and ignore Gemma's investigation.

"Okay…" Waller said tentatively. "Does that mean you're not mad at me?"

"I don't know." Roxy looked him up and down. "You have your moments, especially when you rushed upstairs to rescue Gem. Kind of heroic, that action."

Though Gemma had already thanked her rival, one more hip hip hooray wouldn't come amiss.

"Waller," she said, "you really are a good egg." She thought of how he'd scooped her. "Most of the time."

It was as if he'd read her mind. "Hey, now, Gemma, don't be sore about the story. That's the name of the game. A journalist needs thick skin because, inevitably, you get bitten in the butt by your comrades."

"I'll get over it." And she already had, she thought, telling herself once again that the story hadn't mattered that much, anyway. "Heck, I'm going to march right back into the *Weekly* offices and kick some ass."

That's right. To chase away the agony of failure, she'd decided to become the best damned freaks-and-geeks reporter there was, giving dignity and depth to her stories the likes of which the industry had never seen.

She'd be an ace of mediocrity—and proud of it.

There was no changing what you were meant to be.

Waller pulled up in front of the *Weekly*'s high-rise building, the engine idling. "Then here you go, Gemma. Best of luck."

Since Waller was now a real—no, scratch that—a *daily* reporter for the *Advocate-Tribune,* he wouldn't be coming into the office with her. She wouldn't see him skulking around the lounge anymore. Wouldn't see him working the bar at Cuffs.

She would kind of miss his bumbling big-brother show.

Impulsively, Gemma reached over the seat and hugged Waller. At first, he didn't react. But, slowly, he embraced her back.

"Go get 'em, kid," he said in a ribbity croak.

The guy was a softy after all.

As they disengaged, then smiled at each other, Roxy got out and stood on the sidewalk. Gemma joined her in the post-rain steam of the air.

The older woman laid a hand on Gemma's shoulder. "We'll talk sometime, yeah?"

Gemma nodded, patted Roxy's hand. "I'd like that. I'm going to miss you. Everybody else, too."

"Same here. But you can say some goodbyes tonight. Damien said he'd be out, so I'll see you at Cuffs."

Though Gemma was tempted to abandon the beauty aids she'd left in the bar's storage area, she knew she wouldn't be able to stand herself without facing up to what she'd done. To suck it up and come clean with the people she'd hoodwinked.

"Then I'll see you around nine?" she asked.

"We'll be waiting for you, Gem."

The mention of her undercover name goaded her to rush toward the building, making her itch to change out of the reporter costume and go back to her old life. And, by the time Gemma entered the door, she'd convinced herself that she'd only been gone for a minute, and nothing had changed.

Nothing, except for everything.

"I FEEL TERRIBLE ABOUT WORKING the kid over," Waller said as he guided the car away from the *Weekly*. He'd decided not to clean out his desk until later, after he'd shown Roxy how much he wanted to be with her.

How far he'd fallen for her.

"We all feel a little terrible about something," Roxy said, words heavy with meaning.

She stretched out her bare legs, and while Waller took his fill of them, he almost ran over a tourist who was jaywalking on Poydras Street.

A sweat started to break out on his forehead. Damn, he'd come face-to-face with Theroux today and emerged unscathed. What did he have to be nervous about now?

Anxiety attacked him until Roxy noticed that they'd bypassed Burgundy and were going farther riverside, into the Quarter.

"You taking the long way to Cuffs?" she asked.

Earlier, she'd requested to be dropped off at the bar, telling Waller she needed to work on payroll.

But he had other ideas.

"There's something I want to show you," he said, driving down Decatur to the corner of Ursulines.

He stopped in front of a boarded-up cottage with the memory of coral paint clinging to the walls. A real-estate sign decorated the front.

"What's this for?" she asked.

He cleared his throat. "Just something I ran across yesterday while I was chasing my story. One of my interviews lives down the street, and I saw this on my way to talk with him. I hear from the agent that it's an old café."

At the mention of a café, Roxy's eyes went wistful. She smiled, bursting out of the car to the sidewalk, too excited to even shut the crudmobile's door.

When Waller joined her, he tucked his hands in his pockets, watching closely to see every play of emotion on Roxy's face. She seemed like a child who'd run through the gates of Disneyland for the first time.

"It's out of the way," she said, "but many of the best joints are. Just imagine if I could afford something like this. I could give Café du Monde a real run for their beignets, and then some. Pastries, my *maman*'s recipe for chocolate fudge cake, pralines and good old Creole cooking…" She tried to peek into a slit between a board and a window frame. "And maybe good music, too, huh, Waller? Something for the tourists who stay more than three days, something for the locals."

Waller was so happy that his throat was heating up, expanding, affecting his tear ducts. Not that he was going to weep. Lord knows, Waller didn't do that.

"So you kind of like it, Roxy?"

"Like it?" She whipped around, beaming. "I…"

Uh oh. *She*'d started to cry.

He chanced a few steps toward her, reached out his hand to touch her hair, drew it back in case she was still ticked off at him deep down. "Rox?"

Huffing out a sigh, she shook her head. "I could never buy this. And besides, what would Cuffs do without me? My poor Damien. He's going to need me more than ever now."

This time, Waller did touch her. With all the tenderness in his heart, he stroked the strands of her beautiful hair. Roxy paused, peered up at him with watered-down-whiskey eyes and spiked lashes.

She's going to tell me to knock it off, Waller thought, to go to hell.

He held his breath.

An eternal beat passed as their gazes connected, searching for what was going on between them.

Then, with an explosion of feeling, she leaned forward, seeking to balance herself against his body. Laughing with pure joy, Waller took her into a full embrace, clinging to her, thanking God he'd walked into Cuffs for the wrong reasons.

"Roxy, I'm so sorry for everything."

"Me, too. And you've apologized enough."

"I'll do it a million more times. I just thought you—and everyone—would think so much more of me if—"

She lightly pounded her fists on his back, stopping the litany. "I heard all your explanations during the car ride to the *Weekly Gossip*. No more."

"But—"

Grabbing on to his button-down, she tilted back her head to look up at him, bringing him closer at the same time. "At first, I was angrier than spit, all right, but you know what?" She motioned toward the cottage. "Even while you were getting your story, you couldn't stop thinking of me last night. I don't believe there's ever been a man who showed me such attention."

Not even her husband, he thought, recalling Roxy's small talk about her personal life.

"So you forgive me?"

Roxy played with his shirt, concentrating on the effort. "I do. I'm not sure if Damien will, though. But when all is said and done, I'm glad about this. I hated what was happening to him year by year. There wasn't an end in sight until this happened. I'm angry with you for hurting him—even if you think he came off well— but I'm happy you did it. And then there's your rescue mission for Gem today…"

He'd gone in search of the young reporter and chanced running into Theroux because he'd been concerned about Gemma, not because he'd wanted to impress Roxy.

But he wasn't complaining about the bonus.

"So you kind of admire me?" he asked, urging her on, preening mentally under her compliments.

"Well…" she said, meeting his gaze. "Your bravery did touch me greatly."

He swallowed, willing to take a risk. "And where exactly did it touch you?"

His next heartbeat seemed to last forever while he waited for her answer.

With maddening deliberation, she took his hand, rested it over her breast.

Her heart.

It beat like the wings of a hummingbird beneath his palm. Her soft, rounded flesh sent his temperature skyrocketing. He didn't dare move, wondering if she'd change her mind.

Roxy seemed to sense his uncertainty. With the utmost confidence, she stood on her tiptoes, reached up to bring his mouth down to hers….

And kissed him senseless.

This wasn't like their first encounter—timid, a

yearning quest for permission. No, this kiss had the cleansing power of passion, the rush of two lovers standing under a waterfall while their bodies were soaked and pummeled with need.

Scooping her into his arms, he deepened the contact, running his tongue into her mouth, tasting her spice, amazed at how easy it was to fall into the rhythm of her body pressing into his.

How easy it was to fall into *her*.

As desire pounded his temples, his chest, his groin, he ran his hands up her back, through her hair, then down again until he cupped the lovely, full cheeks of her rear.

She surfaced for air. "I know. Too much good eating. I can go on a diet tomorrow."

"What? Don't you dare." He squeezed her plump butt, loving all the soft skin, loving all of this woman.

Her responding laugh sounded happy, relieved. "Ah, good. I had to promise lots of diets in the past."

"To your husband?" Waller skimmed a worshipful caress up her hips, her thighs. "What a jerk."

"Waller Smith," Roxy said, leaning back, framing his face in her hands. "I think we've got a lot of fine days ahead of us."

His blood gave an ecstatic bump, as if it was nudging him, saying, *I told you so*.

He bent down to kiss her again, just a taste, just once more. Against her lips, he said, "Roxy, I'm not a rich man, but you can see I don't spend money on cars or clothes. I've got a little socked away. Enough to make a down payment on your café."

"You would...?" She bit her lip as the tears returned.

"I will." He traced a finger over her mouth, relaxing her lips, testing their smoothness. "I'm never going to disappoint anyone again, Roxy. Not you, not myself."

Phew. He'd just promised her the world. And it felt great. Felt right. As if he'd always been meant to do it.

"You know I've got two boys still at home," she said. "And there's baggage with me. You realize what you're asking for when you kiss me like that?"

Waller had never been more sure of anything in his life. "I do."

With a heavenly smile, Roxy fell back into his arms, clutching him to her. "Then seal our future, baby. Kiss me until I dissolve."

And he did, right there on a quiet summertime street in front of a deserted building.

Like Waller, the run-down structure would turn out for the better, too.

With the right touch.

THAT NIGHT, OUTSIDE OF CUFFS, Gemma almost talked herself into leaving—for the third time.

She didn't really need to go in, did she? They could keep the makeup, the gel soap and the after-bath splash she'd used before going out with Damien time and again.

Right, she should just go.

Then again, maybe not.

She had to make some apologies to the people she'd befriended, who'd trusted her and unknowingly given her small bits of information. Her conscience demanded it.

With one last exhalation, she pulled open the door. The familiar wash of smoke, liquor fumes, loud conversation and rock and roll tore into her, making her think for one delusional second that she'd returned home.

But that was another falsehood. She was a reporter, not a waitress. A Southern California naïf, not a New Orleans native who knew the ropes. Once again, she felt left behind, swept to the outside of some inner circle she would give her soul to get into.

The bar was crowded tonight, fringed with the hearty laughter of an older crowd—all locals, gathered together for some sort of celebration.

Okay, this wasn't for her.

Just as she turned to leave, Roxy sprinted over, pulling her inside with that how-can-you-resist-me smile.

"Hello!" she said. "We've been waiting for you. And, boy oh boy, do I need to tell you what happened to me!"

Roxy gushed about the plans for her—and *Waller's???*—café while Gemma's old customers shouted out cries of "Gem!" and waved to her. That's right. The ex-cops, everyday heroes and talkative barflies were welcoming her back.

"They're not mad?" Gemma asked.

"Amused, really. Everyone came tonight to show support for Damien and what he's done for the community. He's been getting phone calls from the press all day about interviews. Waller is beside himself because other papers have picked up the story."

A spear of jealousy pierced Gemma, but she tried to ignore the wound. This could have been her glorious day, but at a sacrifice.

Would she have traded Damien for fame?

Irrelevant question. He didn't want her, anyway, and Gemma was keeping her promise to enjoy tabloid journalism by writing about a bayou werewolf now.

The Theroux fiasco had given her more energy, more determination to do her job well. The "werewolf" was intriguing, a wonderfully clever and fascinating man. He'd traveled with a circus most of his life, capitalizing on his copious body hair. Gemma felt for the guy, and was determined to understand why he'd retired and become a hermit. Why he distrusted society but had decided to take money for an interview, anyway.

Much to Nancy's disappointment, Gemma had refused to continue Theroux's story, seeing as how all of the information had been fabricated by her subject, anyway. She'd pounced on the werewolf lead, hoping it would erase Theroux from her mind.

Still… Gemma held back a flood of anguish. It killed her to admit that she wanted to see him again. Talk with him, and feel alive just by being near him.

Nobody had ever challenged her so much, made her reach inside to find the woman beneath her skin.

Gemma summoned a grin for Roxy. "I'm happy for Waller's success," she said, meaning it.

"Gem." Roxy guided her near the stairway, facing her away from the shadowy alcove beneath the steps themselves. "Now that you're here, I need to talk to you about Damien."

Just the sound of his name set her body on fire. "It's over, Roxy, all right? Can we leave it at that?"

A deep male voice sounded from the darkness behind Gemma.

"No, we can't."

Jumping, she rounded on the speaker, heart in her throat and probably in her gaze, too.

Damien stepped into the light, black hair looking tousled, as if he'd been running his fingers through it, pale eyes reaching straight into her.

As Gemma's heartbeat went ragged, she heard Roxy's voice over her shoulder.

"This is what I was getting at," the woman said. "Damien has refused all interviews with the press."

"Except," he said, lasering that perilous, hungry gaze on Gemma, "for one exclusive I intend to give."

She wasn't afraid. Nope. Wasn't terrified of getting rejected by him again.

Meeting his stare, she asked, "What're you talking about, Theroux?"

"You, Gemma. I'm offering you a shot at me. If you'll take it."

He motioned toward the stairs, bringing back the thrill of a forbidden, second-floor-window fantasy at Dante's Basement.

The excitement of reeling in a man who loved revenge more than he could ever love her.

14

As Damien led Gemma to his upstairs office, familiar sounds serenaded her—the creaking floor, the cries of a man and woman having sex behind a closed door.

"*Dieu.*" While Damien sauntered to the occupied room, he motioned with an open palm toward his office. "Please, go in."

The shock still hadn't worn off.

Damien. Here. Now.

Though she hadn't expected to see him again, the jolt of it warmed her, gave her a sense of misguided hope.

Don't, she told herself. When you were downstairs, he explained why he stuck around Cuffs for you. The press is after him, and he knows that going on the record is the only way to make them back off.

She found it funny that Damien Theroux gave a crap about his real image *now*. And even funnier, she wasn't really even focusing on how this interview would answer all of her career prayers.

An exclusive with today's hot headline.

Why wasn't she bouncing off the walls?

Why was she more interested in hearing what he had to say as a person instead of as a subject?

Ignoring his command to enter the office, Gemma leaned against the wall, waiting for him to explain why people were having sex here if it wasn't a cathouse. Waiting for him to reveal every single reason he'd led her to believe it was.

He sheepishly acknowledged her silent rebellion, then banged on the door. The wailing and moaning stopped. Minutes later, a stocky black man with a chest the width of a highway opened the door. He was wearing a sheet around his lower body and a sweaty scowl on his face.

"I'm conducting business," Theroux said.

The man didn't respond, merely trained his gaze on Gemma. Raising his eyebrows, he gave Damien a not-bad-my-friend look, clearly impressed that Gemma was in the hallway.

"Keep it to yourself, Kumbar." Damien walked into his office, leaving the man at the doorway to inspect her.

Gemma returned the favor, recognizing him once again. When a woman with untamed black hair grabbed him from behind and rested her chin on his shoulder, Gemma was doubly sure.

The couple from Dante's Basement. They had seen her in that barely-there peignoir, and they had probably known what was going to happen in the curtainless room.

Somehow, Gemma wasn't embarrassed. There was no shame in fulfilling her fantasies. Not anymore.

"Why, hello, sugar," said the woman, dimpling at Gemma. "Welcome back."

"Thanks."

Gemma performed a smile, then sauntered into

Damien's office, shutting the door behind her. He was sitting in his chair, biding his time.

Where was his arrogance? He seemed stripped of it, with his wrinkled shirt and finger-combed hair. On the desk in front of him was a pair of cards—two aces.

No Dante's Basement flyer. No ledgers.

Just a gambler's hand.

"Not too long ago," she said, "I thought your buddy next door was a customer. That this floor was used for entertainment."

"You were meant to think it." He sounded so exhausted. "His name is Kumbar, my security expert. Kandi is his girlfriend. The two of them certainly didn't mind helping me out with you."

When he motioned to a chair, she sat in it, extracting a notepad, pen and minirecorder from her oversize bag. She was wearing sandals, white linen shorts, a blue silk tank top. Light years away from Gem James's pirate tops and short skirts.

She missed the freedom of wearing sexy clothing. The way it had turned him on.

But now, as he watched her, a flicker of that same attraction lit his eyes. Just a hint, under all that sadness and caution.

Gemma held up the recorder. "You don't mind, do you?"

"Go right ahead. I don't wish to be misquoted."

She chuffed. The skeptical laugh cut through the tense air. "You didn't seem too concerned about misrepresentation a few days ago."

"A lot has changed."

She glanced down at her clean page of notepaper, unable to meet the raw pain of his expression. This was straightforward business, her big chance at success.

Her bruised feelings would only get in the way.

Flicking on the recorder, Gemma took note of the date, time, location and subject. It was as if she'd turned on her ambition, too.

It gave out as much convincing energy as a dying lightbulb.

No matter. She'd get back into the swing of her job, because what else did she have now?

"I guess," she said, "the first thing everyone will want to know is why you used Club Lotus to bring about those reversals of fortune." She set the recording device on the desk between them. "Waller Smith detailed your modus operandi in his article. But creating a club for the sole purpose of taking money from scumbags and giving the proceeds to the people the losers had wronged? Why?"

And why did you keep it a secret? Especially from me, the woman you made love with? Wasn't I important enough?

As he hesitated, Gemma told her inner dumped lover girl to shut up.

"You shoot straight to the point," he finally said.

"Listen." She pointed her pen at him. "If this is going to be another session of dancing around the real answers, I'm not staying. You invited me up here for a reason, Damien. I thought it was because you wanted to come clean."

"I do." He closed his eyes, steepled his fingers under his chin. "It ain't easy."

Swayed by the ache around her heart, she lowered her pen, gave him a moment.

Gathering himself, he lowered his hands to the desk. "I suppose I've nothing left to lose. Everything's gone—my life, my most precious business." He drilled a gaze into her. "You."

Gemma blinked her eyes, asking herself if she had heard him correctly.

"Coming clean doesn't seem like such a bad option in light of all that," he added.

The recorder hummed away on his desk, providing a barrier between them.

He missed being with her? Really?

Overcome, she reached for the recorder, turned it off. Dropped her notepad and pen to the floor by her bag.

"Tell me, Damien," she whispered, wanting so badly to give him another chance. Wanting to run away, just in case the truth would hurt more than his lies. "Please tell me everything."

Relief seemed to consume him as he read her intentions. She would not publish his confessions.

She was willing to sacrifice her dream for him.

Something warmed his eyes, softening them like a candle flaring to life in a dark room.

Then, after a pause, he started.

"Last night," he said, "I talked to you about my parents. But there's no telling you how much I loved them and how much they tried to give me a good life. *Maman* worked in a women's clothing store. My *papa* got hired on with a financial firm in the Central Business District. Even when I was small, I recall him being very excited about this new path for us. He had studied business at the local junior college at nights, and one day, an interview went the right way and he was hired on. He went out to buy new suits and bragged to us during dinner about how big his retirement fund would be, how many shares he owned and how well our family would live. So he invested in our futures, bought a better house in the Marigny than we were used to, even though it'd be years before it could be paid off. But that was no problem for my father. He was going to be with this company for the long run."

Gaze far away, Damien hesitated. "He had such loyalty, that man. Such confidence in the good of people. For years we lived as a happy family. But then he received news that his company had gone bankrupt. The CEOs had cashed out with their own stocks before the business collapsed, and that left the employees with nothing but their own worthless stock options. *Maman* told me not to complain when we moved into a rundown cottage. And even though my father got another decent job, we'd fallen into debt. He was always worried about the future. Always playing catch-up."

Papa Theroux sounded like the salt of the earth, Gemma thought, her heart twisting for a man who felt he couldn't provide for his family well enough. One who had wanted to do so well in his career—just as she had, too.

Damien exhaled, long and slow, eyes narrowing. "My *maman* hid this from me all she could, but *Papa* was getting frustrated. Bitter. Filled with shame because he wanted us to live better.

"Soon…" Damien's voice wrenched on the word, and he bowed his head. Then, he ran a rough hand through his hair, rested his fingers over his eyes. "He couldn't stand the mortification, so he shut himself in the garage one night and left the car's engine on."

Gasping, Gemma moved to the edge of her chair, wanting to touch Damien. But would he just reject her again?

Did it matter right now?

Before she could reach out, he had recovered, standing from his chair, hands in pockets, face stone-cold.

"From then on," he said, "a fantasy took hold in me. A promise that these men—and those like them—were never going to get away with hurting decent people like my father and *maman* again. So I went to Jean Dulac's father…"

He shot her a look that asked if she knew who *exactly* Jean was. With a shrug, Gemma nodded.

Damien didn't react, probably too caught up in containing himself to deal with Gemma's betrayal anymore.

"I convinced him to get me jobs," he continued. "Shuttling winnings from his gaming establishments. Supervising the money laundering. Running a club. I learned everything, made investments with Dulac's help, became a businessman. A year ago, I opened Club Lotus. The first men I bled were the ones who had killed my father."

A chill traveled Gemma's spine, but it wasn't from terror. It was from looking inside Damien's nightmares.

God help her, but she wanted to protect him.

Gemma got out of her chair, daring to approach him. "So you took care of the guilty ones, and more. You gave them what they deserved. But when were you going to stop?"

His smile was filled with self-loathing. "When I was discovered."

Everything came together then, slicing through her mind like a shattered window piecing itself whole again.

Fantasies. Both she and Damien feared—and needed—to get caught.

Having a man love her in the corner of a crowded room...

Making love in front of a window...

Carrying out an act of vengeance and daring people to call you on it...

Though different, each circumstance had exposed them, pushed them further until they'd reached a breaking point.

"I don't understand," she said. "If you wanted to be stopped, if you didn't want to continue what you were doing, even deep down, then why can't you let go of this need to punish those men now?"

He didn't answer.

"God," she said, at the end of her patience. "It just hurts too much to be around you."

He cocked his head. "Am I making your life worse? I thought I made you happy for a time. I thought you got what you wanted from me."

Her voice scratched as she said, "All I *wanted* was something that comes naturally to most people."

He had to know what she meant. Just a kiss.

Just a sign that she wasn't a toy, or a cog in the machine of his revenge schemes.

Still, he held back, fisting his hands at his sides.

This was it, she thought, *the point where I can't fight anymore.*

Damn her for feeling so much for him. For going and falling in love—oh, man, yeah, *love*—with a guy who wasn't capable of the emotion.

And the prize for the Fool-itzer goes to...

Her.

"I can't force you to change," she murmured, turning around to leave—once and for all.

"Gemma, don't go."

It was a plea, a strangled request ripped out of his chest.

She felt his hands on her shoulders, and her world went dizzy as he whipped her around to face him again. Sliding a palm to the back of her head, he crushed her lips to his mouth with the force of long-denied urgency.

A kiss.

Clinging to his shirt, Gemma swayed backward, weak with relief and joy, dismantled by the heat of her ultimate fantasy coming alive.

It was actually happening—everything she'd imagined from the silence of her bed at night. His lips were moving over hers with slick comfort, his hands shaping her to his body, fusing them together and filling the spaces that had always separated them.

In their desperation for each other, they bumped against his desk, jarring a cup of pencils to the floor. He sucked at her, greedy with a hunger she returned, encouraged, enjoyed.

With a whimper, she leaned back her head, struggling for breath, reeling and swaying as he skimmed a hot trail of nips and kisses over her jaw, down her throat.

She threaded her fingers through his thick hair, holding him to her, stumbling backward past the desk, toward the wall, where the velvet couch rested.

This is what she wanted—not a headline whose ink would fade or be erased by tomorrow's news flash. She wanted eternal kisses, the safety of looking into the darkness of an abyss while knowing that she was protected from falling by the man she loved.

She wanted daily challenges, blinding passion.

And someone who would trust her to gently hold their scariest secret near her heart.

When Damien came up for breath, he leaned his forehead against hers, chest heaving. Sweat dampened their skin, washing both of them clean.

"You make me feel as if tomorrow won't be so bad," he said.

Shifting, she smiled against his mouth, cupping his jaw in her hands. "So there's a future?"

Her pulse thudded.

"If you want one," he answered.

He toyed with the strap of her silk top, almost as if asking permission to slide it down her arm. She did it for him, wiggling out of the material, baring her white, lacy bra. As a follow up, she undid her shorts, allowing them to pool around her sandals, which she also took off.

His eyes blazed with rekindled affection as he saw that her answer was yes.

With great care, he unhooked her bra, and she busied herself with his shirt, sliding button after button out of their holes. Soon they were both unclothed, skin glistening under the muted rainbow light of a stained-glass lamp.

Transfixed, Damien explored her with his hands. His arousal grew at the sight of her naked flesh, the feel of her slippery curves, the tiny flinches she responded with when he got close to a sensitive spot.

That kiss still had a hold of him. It had felt so perfect, as if he should have been kissing every day of his life.

But, really, he had been saving that kiss for only one person—Gemma.

This woman would be his bridge, his validation and absolution. She had shown him that control and hatred weren't enough to sustain him, to keep him alive.

There was so much he hadn't known about until she had barged into his life.

Damn, he was anxious. It felt as if someone had plucked daisies in a he-loves-me-he-loves-me-not frenzy, and had released the petals into the air to tickle the lining of his stomach with nerves, desire.

For the first time in his life, he wasn't sure what to do with a woman.

Wasn't sure exactly what he was feeling.

This was rich. He was no more experienced in kisses and tenderness than a virgin in the back of his daddy's car with a prom date.

"What's wrong?" Gemma asked, brushing her fingertips over his belly.

Immediately, his penis stirred, the tip of it prodding her bare thigh.

His first instinct was to return to form, to dominate her with commands and games. But he didn't want to go back there. Not now.

Understanding glowed in Gemma's dark blue eyes, almost as if the kiss had given her the power to enter him and know all his thoughts.

"This is all new for me, too," she said. "Don't worry."

What was new? The scary feelings rattling his pulse? The awareness that he didn't actually own himself anymore because he had given so much to her?

"Believe me," he said, "I'm worried."

Who wouldn't be when they were faced with whatever fever he was suffering?

Was this love? Crazy, out-of-hand, heart-thudding anticipation? The knowledge that he belonged to someone, body and soul?

A slow smile had spread over her lips, just as if she knew how to save him from these mind-scrambling new feelings.

She stood on tiptoe, whispering in his ear. "What's your fantasy?"

Ah, music. Among everything else, she also knew how to make him feel secure.

He smiled, too, then whispered right back.

With a wicked laugh, she pushed him onto the couch, scratched her nails down his chest, his belly, his thighs.

Dammit, he liked that. So did his cock, which was

now straining for attention, the blood pounding into it like the beat of a bass drum.

As he slumped down the velvet, Gemma bent over, flipped her long hair forward, then maneuvered herself so that she could whisk the soft strands, redolent with her lemon shampoo, down the length of his body.

Fascinated, he watched, *felt,* the blond locks, like flames, retreating downward, over his erection. *Merde,* this was killing him with sweet torture, tickling, swirling...

Just beginning.

With her hair hiding her face, Gemma licked his shaft, her tongue like liquid electricity. Damien bucked, groaned, grasped the couch for something to hold on to.

She laughed again. His cock became wet with her kisses as she flicked downward, relishing him, teasing his balls with gentle laves.

"Je t'aime," he said, the moan escaping.

She paused, breath bathing him, hardening him even more, beading his tip with moisture.

"Sorry? What does that mean, Damien?"

Had he really said it? *I love you?*

"Please, Gemma..." His dick was pulsing, needing more of her mouth on it.

She pushed back her hair, sending him a look that established who was in charge and who actually understood enough high-school French to translate. At the same time, she beamed, as if an *I love you* from him was the magic phrase.

Did she feel the same way?

"Damien?" she asked.

He groaned in acknowledgment, unable to do more.

"You'd just better say it again afterward."

And, with that, she took him against her tongue, drenching him with maddening strokes. His hips rocked with her, pressure building within him, pushing at his skin, forcing its way out.

But something elemental caught at his ego. Gemma had mastered him, and he wasn't used to it.

Addled with heat, Damien held back his climax, gathered all his willpower and sat up. In one motion, he scooped her into his arms, turned her around and sat her on his lap. His arousal nudged between her legs, searching, slipping against her juices, her folds.

"Not like this," she said, arching away.

In her own languid change of position, she straddled his hips, bracing her arms on either side of his body as she faced him.

Dammit, he was going to come in a second. He wanted to be in her, be a part of her.

"Face-to-face," she said. "I want you to love me face-to-face."

"Yes," he said, grinding the word out.

"Was that a…?"

"Yes." He grabbed her hips.

"Wait."

He was dying here.

Bending backward to the floor, she stretched an arm toward his pants. A condom. She jerked the material toward her, groping for his wallet.

His body screamed. In reaction, he stroked a hand up the middle of her torso, between the slick valley of her breasts. Cupping one, he kneaded it to a peak. Then, with the same slow-hard ease, he dragged his fingers downward, between the golden thatch of hair between her legs. He could see dew beading there, could see the faint outline of her plumped lips.

With his thumb, he dove between them, circling her clit with gentle pressure.

"Damien," she panted, "you're making this hard."

"That's what I'd say about my cock, too. Hurry."

In seconds, she'd grabbed a foil packet, and he tugged her up to a sitting position as she unwrapped it. Carefully, she coaxed the rubber onto him.

"Happy now?" he said, teeth gritted. He was going to come whether he…

Oh.

She had sheathed herself on him, swiveling her hips to fit him inside of her. Closing her eyes, she moved with him, their pace increasing as he labored under her.

Face-to-face. A beautiful thing.

Spellbound, he watched the play of ecstasy on her features. The flushed skin. The parted lips.

It was like light passing through a window as the sun set, turning a room into another place as the hazy rays revolved to a different angle.

He had kept that particular room, that particular area of himself, locked. It had remained off-limits for so long that he hadn't known the happiness of sharing this—the most intimate of moments—with someone else. Not until now, with Gemma, the woman who would brighten his hidden corners and illuminate his world.

As she churned, leading him to the edge of insanity, Damien thrust into her, causing her to thrash, to grasp his arms, to come to a climax with a wild cry.

Released. Satiated.

But not him. Not yet. She continued, working him with every movement of her hips, pulling him apart like a house crumbling to a fall during a hurricane.

Slam—another section of him pulled into the winds.

Bam—an entire wall ripped into nothing.

Boom—

The last of him was sucked away as everything settled back into place, their hard breathing and collapsed bodies the only reminder of reality.

She snuggled her face into his neck, and he held her tight, afraid she might be carried away, too.

"Je t'aime," she whispered.

He smiled, all too willing to translate.

"I love you," he said, turning his face to hers so he could kiss her again.

And no more words were needed.

Epilogue

Six Months Later

IN A MINT-PAINTED THREE-STORY mansion on Esplanade Avenue, Gemma greeted the morning by opening a box of Roxy's popular beignets that a delivery boy had brought to their door. The scent of fried batter sweetened by powdered sugar and complemented by chicory coffee stirred her, just as much as those birds chirping from the live oaks outside or the cheery splashes from the courtyard fountain did.

Yes, she thought, arranging a plate of the breakfast treats for Damien, this is the life.

Who needed the daily grind of the newspaper? Now she was lucky enough to write from the home in which Damien had been living. His *escape from reality,* as he called it, on these quiet streets of Creole grandeur.

A couple of months ago, the biggest national paper in the country had given her a call. They had noticed her insightful, colorful articles about intriguing local characters. Would Gemma be interested in attempting a weekly syndicated column?

She'd thought about it for two seconds, then said yes. Even though she still wrote about "freaks and geeks"—

a title she was fighting—her parents seemed to accept it. She had told them they'd better, because there was no other choice.

Yes, life was good, as Damien would say.

She carried his breakfast into the parlor to find him shuffling that morning card deck. Even after months of living together, she still found the ritual cute, in a very Damien way.

"What's the hand?" she asked, setting down the platter and clamping her fingers around the ties of her bulky terry-cloth robe. The material draped over her body and to the floor, hiding her feet, trailing around her like a ball gown.

It was so very bellelike. Except for the terry cloth, of course.

He dealt two cards, grinned up at her. "Aces again."

Two of them. It was a record. They showed up at least four times a week.

Taking a beignet in hand, she bent over, fed it to him. Powdered sugar lingered on his lips.

"Damn, that's good," he said, settling back into a Chippendale chair he'd imported for the business.

Much to the delight of Gemma's romantic New Orleans streak, he had decided to sell his other businesses and make a fresh start by importing exotic goods—to cultivate an honest career. The town's elite came to him for furnishings after he and Gemma returned from every scouting trip. Monday, they would be traveling to Bali, just to see what they could discover.

Though she knew the work contented him, sometimes she would still catch him thinking a little too hard, see that dark tilt to his brow. But she always knew how to draw him back.

Gemma leaned over, licked the sweet powder from his lips. He responded with a kiss, deep and passionate.

"Mmm," she said, drawing back, playing with his hair. "Roxy and Waller can really cook, huh?"

"I wouldn't have predicted that Waller would run a decent kitchen, but, yeah. With Roxy's tutelage, they can whip up quite a stomach pleaser."

Damien's fingers brushed against Gemma's as she got up from his lap, going to a glass case that held all manner of weapons. He had found beautifully etched swords and cutlasses on one of their European trips, and he liked to keep the best of his findings for her pleasure.

"Aces," he said, staring at the cards. "They may not be the highest hand in twenty-one, but it's a good start in poker. Switching games would do the trick."

"Aw," she said, taking out one of the cutlasses and inspecting it. "When you find a good game, you should stick to it."

"Maybe so."

Without ceremony, she dropped her robe, heart throbbing through her body in anticipation. When she stepped in front of the man she loved again, a huge, cocky grin lit over his mouth.

God, she loved that grin.

"Pirates," he said, nodding and running an appreciative gaze over her body.

Leather thigh-high boots that kissed the skin of her legs. Very short black shorts. A sword belt dipping over her chest and waist at a jaunty angle. A corset laced over her torso, covering a frilly low-cut top that allowed her breasts to spill out.

She tipped the sword under his chin. "Good morning, my shackled, exotically foreign, bad-man prisoner."

"Mornin'." He raised his eyebrows, just as into the fantasy as she was.

"I'm yer captain, and I command you to submit to a hot bath fer a good scrubbin'. Then…to the chambers with you."

She knew she had him. There was a fire in his eyes, just as hot as the day they'd first met.

When he bounded out of the chair to fling her over his shoulder, Gemma squealed in happiness, dropping the sword.

"I'm in charge 'ere! What're you doin'? Mutiny! Mu-ti-ny!"

Damien lightly spanked her, then headed toward the stairs.

Oh, well, Gemma thought, going along for the ride. Whether he would admit it or not, he was still her prisoner.

And, truth be told, she was definitely his.

Blaze™

 HARLEQUIN® *Blaze*™

Silhouette®

Desire®

Enjoy the launch of Maureen Child's NEW miniseries

THREE-WAY WAGER

The Reilly triplets bet they could go ninety days without sex. Hmmm.

The Tempting Mrs. Reilly
by MAUREEN CHILD

(Silhouette Desire #1652)
Available May 2005

Brian Reilly had just made a bet to not have sex for three months when his stunningly sexy ex-wife blew into town. It wasn't long before Tina had him contemplating giving up his wager and getting her back. But the tempting Mrs. Reilly had a reason of her own for wanting Brian to lose his bet... to give her a baby!